SLUGGERS

TWENTY-SEVEN OF BASEBALL'S GREATEST

George Sullivan

ATHENEUM   1991   New York

Collier Macmillan Canada
Toronto

Maxwell Macmillan International Publishing Group
New York   Oxford   Singapore   Sydney

The following are credits for photographs that appear in
this book without credits in accompanying captions:

National Baseball Hall of Fame and Library pp. 4, 46,
48, 50, 52, 54, 60, 64, 66
Kansas City Royals p. 7
Wide World pp. 10, 12, 14, 16, 18, 20, 24, 26, 28, 34, 36, 44
T.V. Sports Mailbag pp. 32, 38, 42
New York Public Library pp. 56, 58, 68

Atheneum
Macmillan Publishing Company
866 Third Avenue
New York, NY 10022

Maxwell Macmillan Canada, Inc.
1200 Eglinton Avenue East
Suite 200
Don Mills, Ontario M3C 3N1
First edition
Printed in the United States of America

Book Production by Daniel Adlerman

1   2   3   4   5   6   7   8   9   10

Library of Congress Cataloging-in-Publication Data
Sullivan, George, date
Sluggers / by George Sullivan.
p.   cm.
Includes index.
Summary: Profiles twenty-seven of the greatest sluggers
of all time. Includes Sam Crawford, Joe DiMaggio, Reggie
Jackson, and José Canseco.
ISBN 0–689–31566–X
1. Baseball players—United States—Biography—Juvenile
literature.   2. Batting (Baseball)—Juvenile literature.
[1. Baseball players.]   I. Title.
GV865.A1S87   1991
796.357′092′2—dc20
[B]
[920]
90–45817

Contents

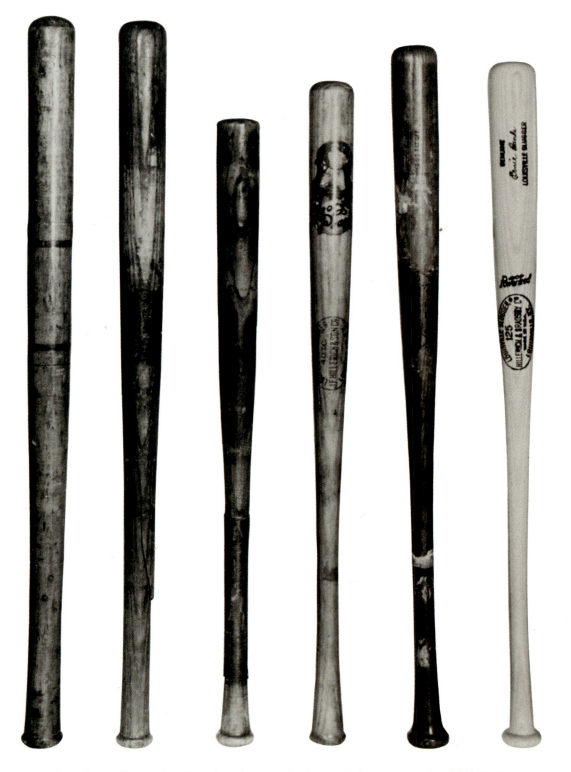

A variety of bats showing the changes in size and shape from the 1870's (far left) to more modern times. Ty Cobb's bat is third from left. Babe Ruth's is fourth. (National Baseball Hall of Fame & Library)

Introduction

When José Canseco of the Oakland A's, who, for sheer power ranks with Mickey Mantle and Willie Mays, comes to the plate, Oakland Coliseum suddenly becomes quiet. "Everything stops," says manager Tony LaRussa, "because everyone wants to watch."

It's much the same at Royals Stadium in Kansas City in the case of Bo Jackson. Every eye is focused on Jackson as he strides toward the plate. By the time he steps into the batter's box, the crowd has usually began to chant, "Bo . . . Bo . . . Bo."

Jackson and Canseco are exciting to watch because they're sluggers. Through the decades, batters who can hit the ball a long distance and do it with some frequency, often providing runs in bunches, have been baseball's biggest heroes. They give the sport much of its color and drama.

It's not just the fans who are attracted to sluggers. The players are, too. "Bo [Jackson] and [José] Canseco are two guys that everyone wants to watch," Seattle catcher Scott Bradley told Pete Gammons of *Sports Illustrated*. "When they're

done, you go to the clubhouse and swap stories about the balls they hit."

Alexander Cartwright, who invented baseball, and Henry Chadwick, another of the game's "fathers," didn't intend that sluggers stand out the way they do today, and for years they did not. Slugging was held in disfavor in baseball's early days. The batter's job was to try to "place" the ball, to slap a base hit through openings in the infield. It was a period of "tight" baseball. Teams played for one run at a time. The idea was to get a base hit, steal second, go to third on a sacrifice or infield out, and race home following another fly.

Of course there were exceptions, such as Roger Connor, Sam Crawford, and a handful of others. But few players ever *tried* to slug the ball. Henry Chadwick did admit, however, that a home run could be "useful" when runners were on base. "Even then," he was quick to say, "we prefer to see a good placer of the ball come to bat, rather than a slugger."

Even if a hitter of the day really wanted to belt the ball, the equipment and rules all but prevented

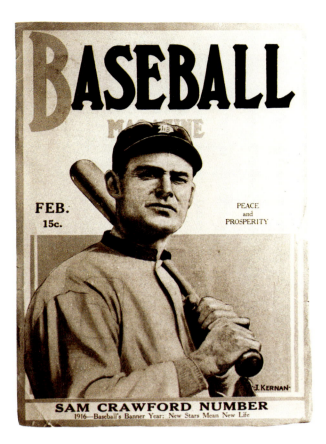

BASEBALL

FEB.
15c.

PEACE
and
PROSPERITY

J. KERNAN

SAM CRAWFORD NUMBER
1916—Baseball's Banner Year; New Stars Mean New Life

In 1902, when Tommy Leach of the Pirates led the National League in homers, he had six. Red Murray of the New York Giants, the league leader in 1909, accumulated seven. In the American League, it was the same. Harry Davis of the A's (who were based in Philadelphia at the time) topped the league for four consecutive years beginning in 1904, and he never had more than 12 home runs in a season.

George Herman ("Babe") Ruth changed things. When Babe Ruth hit a record 29 home runs in 1919, he became the greatest home run hitter in baseball history. But he was just getting warmed up. Ruth smacked an amazing 54 homers the next season, surpassing his own record, in just one year, by 25 home runs! George Sisler of the St. Louis Browns, the runner-up to Ruth, finished with 19 homers.

In addition to hitting 54 home runs that year, Ruth batted .376, scored 158 runs, had 137 runs batted in, and compiled a slugging percentage of .847. Ruth's slugging percentage that year and his home run percentage of 11.8 have never been equaled.

After Ruth's incredible display of power, the *Literary Digest* declared, "Babe Ruth not only has smashed all records, but he has smashed the long accepted system of things in the batting world, and on the ruins of that system has erected another system whose dominant quality is brute force."

Choke hitting, which meant shortening one's grip on the bat with the hope of simply putting the ball into play, was what the *Literary Digest* was referring to when it used the phrase "long accepted system." The great Ty Cobb, who was in his prime when Ruth arrived upon the scene, was a choke hitter. So was Eddie Collins, another outstanding hitter of the day. Everyone copied Cobb and Collins. But, thanks to Ruth, young players everywhere began holding the bat down at the end and swinging for all they were worth.

Ken Williams, a 6-foot, 170-pound outfielder for

it. A pitcher was permitted to doctor the ball about as he wished, scraping it against his cleats or belt buckle, roughing it up with emery cloth or sandpaper. Or he could "load up" the ball with spit or tobacco juice. Trick pitches were the order of the day.

Batters were also hampered by the fact that teams played the entire game with one ball, as long as it stayed in the park. It got lopsided from abuse. It got black, too, from being stained with tobacco juice or whatever else the pitchers happened to be using that day. It got grass stained and mud stained. Late in the game it scarcely resembled the clean, white ball that is served up to hitters today.

It's no wonder that the most famous players of the early 1900s were pitchers. The baseball names that everyone knew were pitchers'—Christy Mathewson, Happy Jack Chesbro, Big Ed Walsh, and Joe McGinnity, all Hall of Famers.

the St. Louis Browns, rather typified what happened. A line-drive hitter, Williams smacked 10 home runs in 1920, which placed him eleventh in the American League. The next year, he decided to modify his batting stance to imitate Ruth. The result was that he more than doubled his homer total, hitting 24. He also added 40 points to his batting average. The next year, 1922, with 39 homers, Williams took the home run title from Ruth, who finished that year with 35.

Some attribute Ruth's record-shattering achievements in 1919 and 1920 to the fact that the makeup of the ball had been changed, that it had been livened up. In fact, during the 1920s, it was often referred to as the "rabbit" ball because it jumped off the bat so briskly.

An important change had taken place in the manufacture of baseballs earlier, when the cork center was introduced in 1910. The following season, batting averages soared. Ty Cobb hit .420 and Cleveland rookie Joe Jackson batted .408. The number of .300 hitters in the American and National Leagues jumped from 16 to 43. But by 1914, averages were back to about where they had been earlier.

However nothing comparable to the addition of the cork center is known to have happened to the baseball in the years before Babe Ruth went on his slugging spree. "The livelier ball may have influenced the situation to some extent," F. C. Lane, editor of *Baseball Magazine* wrote in 1921,

But the livelier ball is a thing so elusive that it offers the scantiest evidence. For example, the manufacturers claim the ball in use last year was no livelier than the ball employed some seasons ago. The manufacturers ought to know what they are talking about, and we can see no reason why they should deceive the public on this point. . . . We are irresistibly impelled, therefore, to see in Babe Ruth the true cause for the amazing advance in home runs.

Ruth and the big hitters that followed him *were* aided by a rule change, however. Late in 1919, the owners of major league teams approved new rules that were meant to eliminate, over time, trick pitches. They outlawed the spitball and such related pitches as the slippery elm ball, the emery ball, and the mud ball. But they didn't outlaw them entirely. Each club was permitted two pitchers who could continue to use these difficult, doctored pitches.

Furthermore, for the 1921 season and beyond, they authorized eight National League and nine American League spitball pitchers to continue to use trick pitches, with no penalty, for the remainder of their careers.

Even in its weakened version, the rule was a boon to hitters. Not only did it mean that some 80 percent of American and National League pitchers were prohibited from throwing trick pitches, it also meant that the balls pitchers threw were almost always clean and white.

The increasing tendency of batters to swing freely, as Ruth did, and not to try placing the ball, plus the ban on trick pitches, triggered a revolution in baseball's offense. Major league teams hit 1,055 home runs in 1922, an increase of 68 percent in a span of five years.

On August 25, 1922, when the Philadelphia Phillies played the Chicago Cubs at Wrigley Field, the game clearly demonstrated what had happened to defense-oriented baseball. The Cubs went into the eighth inning with a 26-9 lead, but just managed to hold on to win, 26-23. The teams made a total of 51 hits.

As this may suggest, hitters of the 1920s not only hit the ball harder and farther than ever before, but they also hit it more frequently. When Ruth hit 29 home runs in 1919 and 54 in 1920, he batted .323 and .376. In 1921, with 59 homers, he hit—incredibly—.378. And when Rogers Hornsby hit 42 homers in 1922 to set a National League record, he batted .401. That year, teams in the

National League had a cumulative batting average of .292. In the American League, it was .285. (In 1988, National League batters averaged .248. In the American League, the average was .259.) In other words, slugging did not result in diminished batting averages, but loftier ones.

With home runs zooming to record levels and batting averages flourishing, people flocked to the ballparks. A record 9.1 million fans attended major league games in 1920. Then, after falling below that mark for three seasons, attendance soared to an average of 9.6 million a season from 1924–1929, and hit 10.1 million in 1930.

Baseball's golden era lasted until the Great Depression of the 1930s, when attendance nosedived. Babe Ruth's departure in 1935 deprived the game of its most colorful player. But new slugging stars—Hank Greenberg, Ted Williams, and Joe DiMaggio—would take over where Ruth left off. The drama and excitement of watching sluggers at bat was here to stay.

During spring training in 1989, Detroit manager Sparky Anderson was asked by Roger Angell of the *New Yorker* to explain how today's players measured up to those of the past. This, in part, was Anderson's reply:

"We don't have a Babe Ruth today, a Willie Mays, or a Mickey Mantle or a Stan Musial, but if you put all *the players in a pot with the old ones, why, the ones today are so superior there's just no comparison. They're bigger, they're quicker—the level of talent is so great now that nobody stands above. They're all giants."*

Anderson didn't mean what he said merely in a metaphorical sense. Today's players are bigger, physically bigger, than those a generation or so ago. "Take a look at photographs of players in the twenties and thirties; they're dinky guys!" Anderson declared. "They'd look like midgets on the field today."

Players of the 1920s and 1930s may not have been exactly "dinky," but they were generally smaller. Among the regulars on the 1939 World Champion Yankees, only two—Joe DiMaggio and pitcher Lefty Gomez—touched 6-foot-2.

Walter ("Rabbit") Maranville, an infielder with the Boston Braves and several other National League clubs, stood 5-foot-5 and weighed 155. His career, which ended in 1935, lasted 23 seasons. There are no Rabbit Maranvilles around today. In the spring of 1990, every pitcher on the roster of the World Champion Oakland A's was 6 feet tall or taller. Most of the eight outfielders were taller than 6-foot-2.

When it comes to sluggers, they're not only bigger today, they're faster. There are hitters who are 6-foot-3 or 6-foot-4, weighing 230 to 240, who can steal bases.

Large speed, as it's called, used to be a rarity. The year he hit 61 home runs, Roger Maris didn't steal a single base. Not one. Willie McCovey had 45 home runs in 1963, and Harmon Killebrew hit

49 in 1964, and neither stole a base.

Of course, there were home run hitters in the past who were capable of stealing bases: Hank Aaron, Willie Mays, and Mickey Mantle are the names that come quickly to mind. When Mickey Mantle hit 54 homers in 1961, the entire Yankee team stole only 28 bases. Mantle's 12 led the club. But there was much less of an emphasis on stealing when they played. All that running could wear out a power hitter. And there was always a chance of injury. What good is a slugger who's on the disabled list?

It's much different nowadays. The best evidence is José Canseco, the first player in baseball history to crack the 40-40 barrier. In 1988, Canseco hit 42 home runs and stole 40 bases.

Canseco puts enormous pressure on the opposition. "He sets up rallies by running," says A's manager Tony LaRussa. "You try to create as many problems as you can for the defense. They just can't play back on the grass when he's on base. One of them has to take the stolen base away, so that opens up a hole."

Several sluggers of the present day have achieved the 30-30 level (30 home runs, 30 stolen bases), and have the potential to duplicate Canseco's 40-40 season. They include Eric Davis, Cincinnati Reds (37-50, 1987); Howard Johnson, New York Mets (36-32, 1987); Darryl Strawberry, New York Mets (39-36, 1987); and Joe Carter, Cleveland Indians (32-31, 1987).

Although they're faster and much more willing to attempt to steal, today's "giants" often have one significant failing: They strike out more. By the time Bo Jackson had completed three full seasons in the major leagues with the Royals, he had 510 career strikeouts. That's 141 more than Joe DiMaggio had in his 13 years with the Yankees.

The most strikeouts Ted Williams ever had in a season was 64, and that was his rookie year. Year in, year out, Darryl Strawberry registers about twice that number.

Even Babe Ruth, who also was regarded as baseball's strikeout king of the 1920s, accumulated 90 only twice, with a career high of 93. By contrast, consider Pete Incaviglia of the Rangers, who, in 1988, became the first player to strike out 150 times in three straight seasons.

Another piece of evidence: Look at the list of top 25 career strikeout leaders on page 00. Fifteen of those players were active in the 1980s.

What's the reason for all the strikeouts? Better pitching is what most observers say. Whitey Ford, the former Yankee star and a Hall of Famer, once observed that when he came into the majors in 1950, his repertoire consisted of a fastball, a slider, and a change-up, which was in the development stage. "That was enough," Ford said. "Now the pitchers are coming out of college and they've got the split-finger, fastballs, sinkers, change-ups, and good sliders. It's a lot different."

And nowadays no one expects a starting pitcher to go nine innings. Every club has an assortment of relief specialists, pitchers who come in from the bullpen and are capable of firing the ball at 93 or 94 miles per hour.

In the age of the strikeout, not every slugger either hits a home run or strikes out and that's it. José Canseco, for example, stays in control when he comes to the plate, just trying to hit the ball hard. "He can hit .290, even in the .300s," says Tony LaRussa. "He's got that good stroke. And he's so strong, that every once in a while, there goes one."

Sluggers such as Canseco, stronger and faster than players of the past, are more than just power hitters. They can also run. With their multiple talents, they've elevated the game of baseball, added an important new dimension to it.

This book features the best sluggers in baseball history. The profiles, which begin with today's players, include the great power hitters of the 1940s and 1950s, Babe Ruth and other sluggers of baseball's Golden Age, and also a handful of heavy hitters representing the scruffy, ragtag days of the turn of the century.

Naturally, statistical information was important in selecting those to be represented. A batter's slugging average, which gives a good indication of the ability to hit for extra bases, was important. The number of homers, triples, and doubles was another consideration.

Consistency was an element too. Baseball history is littered with one-season and two-season sluggers. To be included, a player had to prove himself a slugger over an extended period.

And as much as any of these, players were evaluated on the basis of that special quality of being able to stir the fans, to generate excitement and drama by merely stepping into the batter's box. Babe Ruth could do that. So could Joe DiMaggio and Willie Mays. So do José Canseco and Bo Jackson.

Bo Jackson

Born: November 30, 1962; Bessemer, Alabama
Height: 6'   Weight: 185
Bats right-handed, throws right-handed

With every swing of his bat, there's a chance Bo Jackson will do something extraordinary. So when he steps to the plate, everyone watches.

The fans know that his first major league home run, hit in September 1986, went three quarters of the way up the outfield embankment at Royals Stadium in Kansas City and hit the grass so hard it stuck. They know that in his first All-Star game at bat in 1989, he golfed the second pitch beyond the center field fence at Anaheim Stadium, 448 feet from home plate.

The fans remember his confrontation with Nolan Ryan in May 1989 too. Jackson had struck out six consecutive times against Ryan. When he faced him a seventh time, the Rangers' fastballer knocked Jackson down with a pitch. Two pitches later, Jackson hit a home run that measured 461 feet.

Jackson's defensive skills are impressive too. In a game at Seattle in 1989, speedster Harold Reynolds of the Mariners was racing home with what he thought would be the winning run on Scott Bradley's double off the left field wall. Jackson grabbed the bouncing ball off the wall and, in one motion, turned and threw home. The ball never bounced in its 300-foot flight. It sailed into catcher Bob Boone's glove and Reynolds was out. Even after he had seen the replay, Reynolds couldn't believe what had happened.

It's not just the fans who find Jackson exciting. So do the players. "Players from both teams watch when Bo takes batting practice," according to Kansas City pitcher Bret Saberhagen. "There's always a feeling you're going to see something you never saw before and we don't want to miss it."

If sports statisticians had a category titled Most Extraordinary Feats, the young man who plays left field and bats cleanup for the Royals would be the major league leader. He's been a world-class sprinter, won the Heisman Trophy as a running back for Auburn, and walked off with the MVP honors in the All-Star game.

When Jackson announced in 1987 that he planned also to play professional football for the Los Angeles Raiders after the baseball season, calling football a "hobby," he shook up the Royals management. They felt Bo could become one of baseball's all-time greats—if he stuck to baseball.

In one of his first games for the Raiders, Bo ran 221 yards, including a 91-yard touchdown run from scrimmage, the eighth longest in National Football League history. His yards-per-carry average is one of the league's highest. In a two-touchdown game against the Bengals in 1989, he gained 159 yards on 13 carries, 12.2 yards per attempt.

One of eight children born to a Bessemer, Alabama, steelworker and his wife, Bo was named Vincent by his mother and nicknamed Boar by a cousin, who said he "was as tough as a wild boar." The nickname was shortened to Bo in high school.

The Jacksons were very poor. Says Bo: "I realized early on that I was starting at the bottom." A bully as a young boy, Bo and his gang ran in the streets, threw stones through store windows, and stole kids' bikes. In high school, Bo turned to

When Jackson gets ready to hit, a rustle of anticipation fills the stadium. (Kansas City Royals)

Coach Doug Rader, California Angels manager, congratulates Jackson as he rounds third and heads for home after blasting a home run in the first inning of the 1989 All-Star game at Anaheim Stadium. (Wide World)

sports, setting state and national records in track, baseball, and football. College coaches begged Bo to come to their schools. He chose Auburn University in the little town of Auburn, Alabama. There he excelled in baseball and football. "He's got as much talent as Mickey Mantle or Willie Mays," said Dick Eagan, a big league scout.

After college, Bo turned down $3 million from the NFL's Tampa Bay Buccaneers to play baseball for Kansas City. His salary with the Royals was a modest $200,000.

How could you turn down $3 million, Bo was asked. "In life, you take chances," he answered. "My first love was baseball rather than football. My goal is to be the best baseball player Bo Jackson can be."

A bright future looms for Jackson. "The more he plays, the better he gets," teammate George Brett said in 1989. "Just look at the improvement he made from his rookie year to last year and from last year to this year. I think we've seen only a portion of the greatness he's going to give us."

"The more he plays, the better he gets," said teammate George Brett of Jackson. (Wide World)

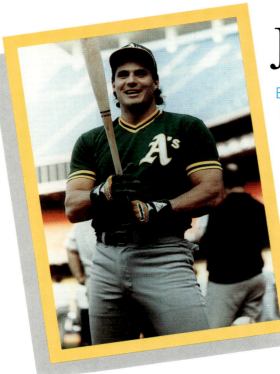

José Canseco

Born: July 2, 1964; Havana, Cuba
Height: 6'3"   Weight: 230
Bats right-handed, throws right-handed

At the age of 25, muscular José Canseco of the Oakland A's was already being hailed as one of baseballs brightest stars, an astounding mix of power and speed. In 1988, Canseco became the first player to hit 40 home runs and steal 40 bases in the same season. He hit .307 and led the league in slugging. Little wonder that he was the unanimous choice as the American League's MVP.

Rival managers have a tough problem with Canseco. They don't want to get beat by a home run. They also know a walk plus a steal is like a double. "Canseco adds a whole new dimension to the game of baseball," says Seattle manager Jim Lefebvre. "He's special."

There was little in José's early life to suggest he was going to be a baseball superstar. He and his twin brother, Ozzie, had little interest in sports of any kind until they were 12. José was a splendid high school player at Coral Park in Miami, yet not good enough to be named to the 1982 Florida high school all-star team, which included such future major leaguers as Dwight Gooden of the Mets and

Mike Greenwell of the Red Sox. "Canseco had a great swing but he was small, and often Latin kids don't get any bigger after high school," said Red Sox scout George Digby.

The A's waited until the fifteenth round of the 1982 high school draft to pick Canseco. Right after he signed, he started to sprout. "I was a late bloomer," he says. And thanks to a vigorous weight-training program on which he embarked, he began to add muscle.

In the minor leagues, where he continued to build his strength, Canseco won renown with his monstrous home runs. In 1985, at 6-foot-3, 225 pounds, he put together a big year, which included 41 homers, most of them coming with Huntsville (Alabama) in the Southern League. In 1986, he made it to the majors, where he wound up as Rookie of the Year after hitting 33 homers, driving in 117 runs, and stealing 15 bases. In his sophomore season, his stats were similar—31 home runs, 113 RBIs, and again 15 stolen bases.

The following year, 1988, Canseco decided to

try something different. "Guys with power, a lot of them, rely on power alone," he said. "I didn't want to be one of those guys."

Three weeks into the season, he dropped a bombshell. "I think I can hit 40 home runs and steal 40 bases this year," he said. "I'm going to go for it."

Eleven players in baseball had achieved the 30-30 level but no one had ever reached 40-40. When Canseco attained that plateau by stealing his fortieth base in Milwaukee on September 23, he seemed more relieved than elated. "I didn't want to end up short and say I stuck my foot in my mouth," he said.

"Some people would like to think I've gone as far as I can go," Canseco says. "But when you start to think that way, that's when you defeat yourself. I want to cut down on my strikeouts and I know I can hit for average. And I want to be a smarter player, too." If those are goals that Canseco sets for himself, very few people doubt he will achieve them.

Canseco gives a high five fist to teammate Dave Henderson following a Canseco home run against the Boston Red Sox in the American League Championship Series in 1988. (Wide World)

Canseco belts homer number 40 against the Kansas City Royals in September 1988, on his way to becoming the first player in major league history to record 40 homers and 40 steals in a season. (Wide World)

George Brett

Born: May 15, 1954; Glen Dale, West Virginia
Height: 6'   Weight: 195
Bats left-handed, throws right-handed

*W*alk *him. That's the only defense against that fellow. Honestly. I'm considering walking him every time he comes up against us. . . .*

> Sparky Anderson
> Manager, Detroit Tigers

Taking everything into consideration, his great abilities plus the intangibles, Brett is probably the best player in the game today.

> Gene Mauch
> Former Manager, California Angels

If God had him no balls and two strikes, he'd still get a base hit.

> Steve Palermo
> American League Umpire

That's how they talked about George Brett during the 1980s, when he ranked as one of the game's outstanding hitters, if not its most outstanding. During that decade, Brett won a couple of batting championships, led the American League in slug-ging three times, and almost always managed to hit 20 to 30 homers.

The league's MVP in 1981, Brett typified the new breed of slugger. He was patient, selective, and smart, a master of his craft.

To appreciate Brett's quick swing and ability to hit the ball hard, consider a league championship game in 1985, Kansas City versus Toronto. The Blue Jays never got Brett out. He hit two home runs, a double, and a single. He drove in three runs and scored four, including the winning run in the Royals' 6-5 victory.

Toronto pitchers shook their heads in disbelief. Brett hit whatever they threw. The home runs came off of a change-up down and in, and a fastball up and away. His double, which missed clearing the right field wall by inches, was hit off of a slider. His single, which was just out of reach of the second baseman, was hit off of a forkball.

"George is the best situation hitter I've ever seen," his teammate, Hal McRae, said after that performance. "Reggie [Jackson] was a home run

At the plate, Brett is patient and smart, with a quick swing and the ability to hit the ball hard.
(Wide World)

situation hitter. But if he didn't hit a home run, he struck out. George can get you whatever you need."

In his early years as a professional, there was nothing special about Brett. After being drafted by the Royals in 1971, he bounced around the minor leagues for three years. In 1974, when he was finally assigned to Kansas City, manager Jack McKeon platooned George, using him only against right-handed pitching.

George's problem was that he was strictly a pull hitter, trying to slam every pitch over the right field fence. Charlie Lau, the Royals batting coach, admired Brett's swing and believed he could help him to improve. Lau convinced Brett that in order to become a good hitter he would have to stop trying to pull the ball and learn to "go with the

pitch." Before long, George was spraying line drives to every part of Royals Stadium.

In 1976, Brett, with a .333 average, led the league in batting for the first time. In 1980, he led again, batting .390.

George was born in Glen Dale, West Virginia, and brought up in El Segundo, California, a town where bumper stickers used to say, BASEBALL CITY, USA. George and his three older brothers practically lived on the baseball fields of Recreation Park during the summer. Their dad often handled the PA system for games while Mrs. Brett sometimes worked at a concession stand.

All four of the Brett boys became professional players. Two made the majors and were World Series performers. One is going to wind up in the Hall of Fame.

Mike Schmidt

Born: September 27, 1949; Dayton, Ohio
Height: 6'2"   Weight: 200
Batted right-handed, threw right-handed

Season after season during most of the 1970s and all of the 1980s, Mike Schmidt not only produced for the Philadelphia Phillies, but produced when the team needed him to produce.

His 500th career home run was no mere ceremonial blast. It won a game in Pittsburgh. In the club's pennant race in 1980, Schmidt's homer against the Montreal Expos clinched the division title. In the World Series against the Kansas City Royals that year, Schmidt batted .381, smacked two home runs, drove in seven runs, and was chosen the MVP as the Phillies won the Series for the first time in the franchise's 106-year history.

Schmidt, who spent his entire career with Philadelphia, was born and brought up in Dayton, Ohio. After graduating from Fairview High, he went on to Ohio University in Athens, Ohio, playing shortstop for a team that reached the College World Series. The Phillies made him their second choice in the 1971 free agent draft.

His rookie season is one Schmidt would like to forget. Always trying to crush the ball, he hit .196

and struck out 136 times. He realized he was going to have to change his attitude and develop what he called a "natural stroke," hitting line drives like Pete Rose. "Rose stings the ball three times a game," said Schmidt. "That's the kind of hitter I want to be."

The next season, Schmidt's attitude was different. He said: "Instead of trying to hit every pitch with every ounce of strength, I tried to pick out a good pitch and swing naturally, letting the home runs take care of themselves." It worked. The new Schmidt led the league in homers that year, 1974, with 36. He went on to be the league's home run leader eight times during his career, smacking a total of 548.

Schmidt often displayed awesome power. In batting practice at Veterans Stadium, he once hit a ball so hard it shattered a section of supposedly bullet-proof Plexiglas atop the left field fence.

Another time, in a game against Houston at the Astrodome, Schmidt belted a 340-foot drive off a public address system loudspeaker that hung 117 feet above the playing field. Someone calculated the ball would have traveled 600 feet if its flight hadn't been interrupted. All Schmidt got out of it was a ground-rule single. The next day the loudspeaker was raised.

Schmidt was highly praised for his defensive skills too, winning ten Gold Gloves as the National League's top third baseman. "No other third baseman ever did what he did with both his bat and his glove," wrote Dave Anderson in the *New York Times*. "Not Brooks Robinson, not Eddie Mathews, not Pie Traynor."

Schmidt missed the last two months of the 1988 season with a shoulder injury. The following season was a struggle. Late in May, Schmidt was batting .203 with only six homers. Then, in a 3-3 game in San Francisco, he booted an easy grounder. It was the kind of play Schmidt knew he once would have been able to make routinely. When the next hitter homered, sending the Phillies down to defeat, Schmidt suddenly decided he didn't want to play baseball anymore. A week later, Schmidt bid an emotional farewell to the game.

Schmidt watches the flight of his 535th career homer during a game against the Padres in San Diego in 1988. (Wide World)

Reggie Jackson

Born: May 18, 1946; Wyncote, Pennsylvania
Height: 6'   Weight: 195
Batted left-handed, threw left-handed

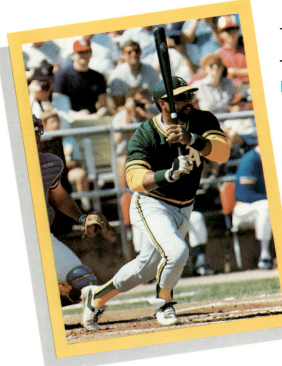

Three different pitchers, three first pitches, three home runs. Not since Babe Ruth had anyone slugged three home runs in one World Series game. And not even Ruth had ever managed five in one World Series—as Reggie Jackson did in 1977 in wrapping up the world title for the New York Yankees. It was one of the most amazing displays of power in Series history.

Reggie Jackson was always at his best in World Series competition. Mr. October he was called. His Series slugging percentage of .755 is the best ever. His Series batting average of .357 is the ninth best.

Fans loved Jackson. Or hated him. When he came to the plate, every eye was on him. And often his plate appearances were accompanied by the chant—"Reg-gie . . . Reg-gie . . . Reg-gie."

Born and brought up in a Philadelphia suburb, one of seven children, Reggie was a three-sport star at Cheltenham High. Besides playing baseball, he ran dashes in track and played halfback on the football team. His baseball skills earned him a scholarship to Arizona State University. After two

years there, he was drafted by the Kansas City Athletics in 1966, receiving $95,000 in bonus money. Jackson spent less than two seasons in the minors before becoming a starting outfielder for the A's, who were based in Kansas City until 1968.

Jackson helped the A's, in Oakland now, win the World Series in 1973, 1974, and 1975. He was named the league's MVP in 1973 when he batted .293, hit 32 homers, and drove in 117 runs.

When Jackson refused to sign a contract in 1976, Oakland owner Charles O. Finley, a stubborn man, shipped his controversial star to the Baltimore Orioles. At the end of the 1976 season, Jackson joined baseball's first group of free agents, then signed a five-year, $2.6 million contract with the Yankees.

Even when he paced the Yankees to the pennant drive in 1977, Jackson was seldom far from controversy. In the final pennant playoff game, manager Billy Martin benched Jackson for his nonchalant defensive play. Reggie later delivered the key pinch hit in that game.

Yankee owner George Steinbrenner eventually

became disenchanted with his star and dealt Reggie to the California Angels in 1982. Reggie tied with Gorman Thomas of the Milwaukee Brewers for the league lead in homers that year, with 39, and the Angels were division champions. The Yankees finished fourth. Steinbrenner later admitted trading Jackson was a mistake.

During his career, Jackson won four home run crowns (two were shared) and was the league's slugging leader three times. But he also struck out more than any other player in history. He fanned 2,597 times, about once in every four at bats. No other player is close to that record.

"I've been called egotistical, selfish, uncaring, even sadistic," Jackson once said. "Things have been said and written that are humiliating to me."

But Jackson didn't complain too loudly. Pete Axthelm of *Newsweek* once asked him: "If you had to choose between criticism and being ignored, which would you prefer?"

"Being ignored," Reggie answered, "would be pretty awful."

Jackson was the American League's slugging leader three times. But he also struck out more than any other player in history. (Wide World)

Willie McCovey

Born: January 10, 1938; Mobile, Alabama
Height: 6'4"   Weight: 205
Batted left-handed, threw left-handed
Elected to the Hall of Fame in 1986

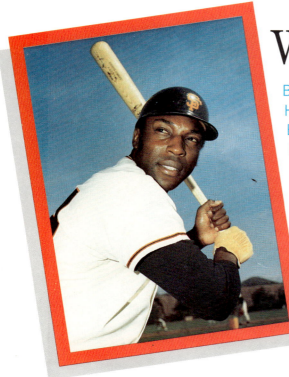

Willie McCovey, a San Francisco landmark for almost two decades, blasted 18 grand slams, a National League record, and won or shared home run titles in 1963, 1968, and 1969. But according to McCovey himself, the hardest ball he ever hit was an out. The scene was Candlestick Park, the seventh game of the 1962 World Series. The Giants trailed the Yankees, 1-0. It was the ninth inning, two outs, McCovey at the plate with the tying run on third, the winning run on second. McCovey swung hard and drilled a scorching line drive right into second baseman Bobby Richardson's glove.

That Series-ending line drive wasn't the only thing San Francisco fans were unhappy about. Earlier in the season, when McCovey had been shifted from first base to the outfield to make room for Orlando Cepeda, he had not been an instant success. More than a few times, boos and catcalls rained down upon him.

But McCovey never gave up on himself. He became a capable outfielder and, using a whippy 34-ounce bat that he adopted on the advice of Ted

Williams, an idol of the fans, McCovey walloped 521 homers during his career. No National League left-hander has hit more. Three times he led the league in slugging.

The seventh of a family of 10 children, McCovey grew up in Mobile, Alabama, the city that was also the home of Hank Aaron. Aaron played baseball in grammar school and high school, but McCovey's high school had no team. He had to learn the game on Mobile sandlots, and barely earned a Giant contract.

McCovey broke in with the Giants in 1959 with a perfect 4-for-4 game against Philadelphia ace Robin Roberts. He hit .354 that year to capture Rookie of the Year honors.

McCovey's reputation for power came later. At the plate, he spread his feet wide apart, dipped his left shoulder, and waved his bat like a menacing war club. Manager Gene Mauch called him "the most awesome hitter I've ever seen."

Although he was quiet and shy in his first years with the Giants, McCovey became a friendly and talkative team leader, noted for his skill as a public speaker. Of San Francisco, he once said, "I've never felt I belonged anywhere else." The fans returned his affection. He became a civic institution, like the Golden Gate Bridge or the little cable cars. When he was traded to San Diego in 1974, attendance at Candlestick Park took a nosedive. When he returned to the team in 1977, a sellout crowd gave him a five-minute standing ovation. McCovey showed he was glad to be back by banging out 28 homers and batting in 86 runs that season to win the National League's Comeback Player of the Year award.

Like Ted Williams, for whom he had great admiration, McCovey cultivated, not a level swing, but a slight upswing with the hips leading. By coinci-

Of San Francisco and the Giants, McCovey once said: "I've never felt I belonged anywhere else." (Wide World)

dence, when he retired after 22 seasons, McCovey's total of 521 homers just equaled that of Williams.

McCovey is congratulated at home plate by teammate Darrell Evans after McCovey belted his 489th career homer, putting him thirteenth on the all-time homer list.   (Wide World)

Hank Aaron

Born: February 5, 1934; Mobile, Alabama
Height: 6'   Weight: 180
Batted right-handed, threw right-handed
Elected to the Hall of Fame in 1982

In what was perhaps the longest dramatic pause in sports history, Hank Aaron of the Atlanta Braves finished the 1973 season with 713 career home runs, one short of baseball's most notable record, the 714 homers hit by Babe Ruth. A whole winter of anticipation followed.

Once the season began, with Atlanta at Cincinnati, Aaron wasted no time. On his very first time at bat, facing Jack Billingham, Aaron socked a sinking fastball over the left center field fence. Now he and Ruth were tied.

In Atlanta four days later, on April 8, 1974, at exactly 9:07 P.M. EST, before 52,775 fans who were there to see history made, Hammerin' Hank lifted an Al Downing fastball over the left center field fence where it was caught in the Braves bullpen by relief pitcher Tommy House.

House jogged in to deliver the ball to Aaron. By the time he got to home plate, a huge crowd had gathered. When House found Aaron, he was being hugged by his mother and looking over her shoulder. "Hammer, here it is," House said, and he put the ball in Aaron's hand.

"Thanks, kid," Aaron said, and he reached out to touch House on the shoulder. "I looked," House said, "and saw what many people have never been able to see in him—deep emotion. He has such cool. He never gets excited. And, I looked, and he had tears hanging on his lids. And then it was brought home to me what the home run meant, not only to him but to all of us."

After Aaron clouted his 715th home run, later voted the most memorable in baseball history, he kept right on hitting them. When he retired in 1976 after 23 major league seasons, his homer total had reached 755.

Aaron's awesome feat in eclipsing Babe Ruth's home run record has served to overshadow many other of his accomplishments. At the time he retired, he was not only the all-time leader in homers but also in runs batted in; he was the runner-up in runs scored and total hits (Pete Rose, in becoming the all-time hit leader, would later top Aaron).

Four times Aaron led the league in home runs in 1957, 1963, 1966, and 1967; But his highest total, 47, came in 1971 and was only one home run short of Willie Stargell's league leading 48. Four times he led in RBIs; four times he led in slugging. Twice he led the National League in batting average. In 1957, when the Braves won the World Series, Aaron was the National League's MVP.

The second of seven children, Henry Aaron was born and brought up in Mobile, Alabama. He fell in love with baseball as a kid. When he wasn't playing the game, he was watching it. Stan Musial was the player he admired the most. By the time Aaron reached high school, he had made up his mind he was going to be a professional baseball player.

When he was 17, Aaron signed a contract with the Indianapolis Clowns of the Negro American League. He tore apart the league pitching. When his batting average soared to .450 and above, major league scouts started following the Clowns. The Braves, based in Milwaukee at the time, made him the best offer, and by midseason he was playing for Milwaukee's minor league team in Eau Claire, Wisconsin, in the Class C Northern League.

Aaron was slender and did not look like a power hitter. And he hit off his front—his left—foot, something no instructor would ever teach. But Aaron had the ability to wait until the last split second before lashing the bat around. His quick wrists were what were to get him all those home runs.

Even at this stage of his career, Aaron could hit about any pitch anywhere. He seemed to have no weaknesses at the plate. Once, when he was playing for Eau Claire, a rival manager ordered his pitcher to brush Aaron back. In came a fastball less than two inches from Henry's nose. Aaron

In 1976, when he broke Ruth's record, Aaron used a 36-inch, 37 ½-ounce bat, the heaviest of his career. (George Sullivan)

"I'm going to let the umpires handle the balls," Aaron said early in his career, "and I'll handle the strikes." (Wide World)

promptly belted it into center field for a double. "I give up," the manager said. When brought up to Milwaukee in 1954, Aaron was a solid success, batting .280 and rapping 13 homers, and ending up as the team's most valuable player.

In the years that followed, the most remarkable feature of Aaron's career was his consistency, his ability to produce day after day for 23 seasons. Seldom was he sidelined by injury or ill health. For the 20 years beginning in 1954, his rookie season, Aaron averaged 564 at bats per season. Among all players, Aaron ranks second in at bats (behind Pete Rose). Babe Ruth is 65th on the list. Ruth had 8,399 at bats; Aaron, 12,364.

As further evidence of his consistency, consider that Aaron hit 40 or more home runs eight times, the last time when he was 39 years old.

Several months before Babe Ruth died in 1948, he spent a day with Frederick G. Lieb, editor of the *Sporting News,* who interviewed him on several different subjects, including Ruth's home run records.

"Somebody will break my record of 60 homers in a season," Ruth rightly predicted. But the Babe felt his career homer record was safe. "No one will ever come close to my lifetime 714 homers," Ruth said to Lieb. Of course, Ruth made that statement without ever having known anyone the likes of a young man named Henry Aaron.

Not long after his final season, Aaron's 44 was retired by both the Atlanta Braves and Milwaukee Brewers. (George Sullivan)

Harmon Killebrew

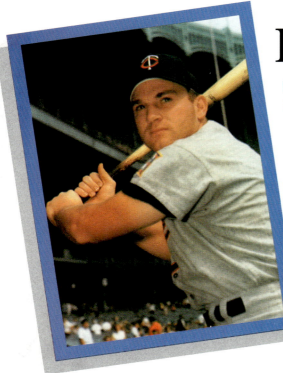

Born: June 29, 1936; Payette, Idaho
Height: 6'   Weight: 200
Batted right-handed, threw right-handed
Elected to the Hall of Fame in 1984

When Ossie Bluege, a scout for the Washington Senators, journeyed to Payette, Idaho, in the summer of 1951 to get a line on 16-year-old Harmon Killebrew, Bluege saw the young man "hit the ball a country mile over the left field fence." When the game ended, Bluege persuaded the club to leave the lights on so he could measure how far the ball had traveled. A tape measure disclosed the distance to be 435 feet. Soon after, Bluege signed Killebrew for the Senators.

In his 22-year major league career, Killebrew made his living "hitting the ball a country mile." He didn't go in for lofty batting averages. His highest for one year was .288, and for his career he managed to hit no more than .256.

Speed wasn't Killebrew's specialty, either. He never got the bunt sign and he stole merely 19 bases in his 22 seasons. In fact, Killebrew established the major league record for seasons without a stolen base—three. And Killebrew played the outfield, first base, second base, and third

base without anyone ever giving him a Gold Glove award.

All that didn't matter. What Killebrew could do was hit home runs, hit them farther and with much greater frequency than only a handful of sluggers in baseball history.

In 1954, when he was 18, Killebrew went directly from high school to the major leagues. The first major league game he ever saw, the Senators versus the White Sox, was one in which he played as well. He went in as a pinch runner. "I wondered what I was doing there," he once recalled.

From 1954 until 1958, Killebrew, used as a pinch hitter and utility infielder, shuttled back and forth between the Senators and assorted minor league teams. In 1959, his first full year with the club, he belted 42 homers to share the league lead with Rocky Colavito of Cleveland. In the field, he began at second base, played the outfield for a time, and ended up at first.

Year in and year out, home runs boomed off his

Killebrew put his powerful wrists, arms, and shoulders into every swing.
(Wide World)

bat—46 in 1961 (the year the Senators moved to Minnesota and became the Twins), 48 in 1962, 45 in 1963, 49 in 1964, 44 in 1967, and 49 in 1969. In each of those seasons, except 1961, he either led or tied for the league lead in homers, for a total of six league-leading seasons.

In 1965, at 29, Killebrew had a banner season. Although his 39 homers did not lead the league, he had 140 RBIs and was named MVP. (The Twins won the pennant but fell in seven games in the World Series to the Los Angeles Dodgers and their strong pitching.)

For his career, Killebrew clouted 573 homers.

He is number five on the all-time list. Babe Ruth is the only American Leaguer who ranks higher.

Was Killebrew feared? Well, he holds the all-time record for intentional bases on balls—160.

Killebrew was sometimes called Killer. But the nickname didn't fit his gentle nature. When he was being inducted into the Hall of Fame in 1984, he became very emotional. Several times he choked up in recalling the encouragement he had received in his early years from his late father and 89-year-old mother. Harmon Killebrew was violent and dangerous, a killer, but only if you happened to be a pitcher.

Eddie Mathews

Born: October 13, 1931; Texarkana, Texas
Height: 6'1"   Weight: 190
Batted left-handed, threw right-handed
Elected to the Hall of Fame in 1978

Throughout his 16-year career, the home run was Eddie Mathews's trademark. Handsome and muscular, the left-hand hitting Mathews was the seventh player in baseball history to collect 500 homers. Beginning in 1953, he hit 30 or more home runs for a record nine consecutive seasons, and hit over 40 homers four times, winning titles with 47 in 1953 and 46 in 1959.

Despite these and other gaudy achievements, Mathews never achieved the celebrity status of Mickey Mantle, Willie Mays, or some of his other contemporaries. One reason was because he played for the Braves, moving with the team from Boston to Milwaukee in 1953, and then to Atlanta in 1966. (Mathews is the only player ever to play for one team in three different home cities.) And the Braves' attack was usually led, not by Mathews, but by a quiet and modest outfielder with tremendous power by the name of Hank Aaron.

Mathews hit third in the Braves' lineup, Aaron fourth. The two gave the team an unparalleled one-two punch. They combined for 863 homers as teammates between 1954 and 1966, a total that puts them ahead of Willie Mays–Willie McCovey (800) and Babe Ruth–Lou Gehrig (772).

When Mathews was 17 and playing American Legion baseball in Santa Barbara, California, and was offered the chance to play pro ball, he didn't hesitate. At one minute after midnight on the day he earned his high school diploma, which made him eligible to sign a baseball contract, Mathews left his high school prom in Santa Clara, California, to discuss salary terms with a Braves scout. Not long after, in his first at bat in the minor leagues, he homered. And in 1952, as a 20-year-old rookie for the Braves, he hit three home runs one afternoon in a game against the Giants at New York's Polo Grounds. No rookie had ever homered three times in a game. That season Mathews topped the major league rookie record for third basemen by slamming 25 homers.

In 1953, the Braves moved from Boston to Milwaukee, where the handsome Mathews was greeted enthusiastically. That year, at 21, he belted

Mathews takes off, his bat in the air, his eyes on a ball that was headed out of the park for his fifteenth homer of the 1960 season. (Wide World)

Mathews loses his footing in an attempt to field a line drive in a game against the Giants at Candlestick Park in 1960. (Wide World)

47 homers to lead the National League and set a Braves' record (which was tied in 1971 by Aaron, when the team was in Atlanta).

During the early 1950s, Mathews was often hailed as "the National League's Mickey Mantle." He drove in over 100 runs five times and scored more than 100 eight times.

Some of Mathews's warmest memories as a player go back to the 1957 World Series, the Braves versus the New York Yankees. In the bottom half of the tenth inning of the fourth game, with the Yankees leading, 5-4, Mathews thrilled the crowd with a mammoth line drive to deep left field that barely landed foul. Then he pulled another blast to right field, but that also was foul. Finally, after taking two pitches for balls, he sent another towering drive to right, which stayed fair, giving the Braves a 7-5 win that evened the Series. In the fifth game, he singled off Whitey Ford and scored the game's only run.

But Mathews is proudest of a fielding play he made in that Series. With two out in the ninth inning of the seventh and deciding game, Moose Skowron lined a shot down the third base line. Mathews dived to his right to spear the ball, jumped to his feet, and stepped on third to end the Series. "That play ranked right up there with breaking the 500-homer barrier," Mathews said.

"I'd made better plays, but that big one in the spotlight stamped me the way I wanted to be remembered."

After he retired as a player in 1968, Mathews coached and managed the Braves. In fact, he was the team's manager in 1974, the year that Hank Aaron surpassed Babe Ruth's career record of 714 homers. "Very few people could have handled the pressure as well as Hank did," Mathews said. "I had problems with it and I was just the manager."

Mathews and Aaron combined to form what was baseball's most successful one-two punch, smacking 863 homers as teammates between the years 1954 and 1966. (Atlanta Braves)

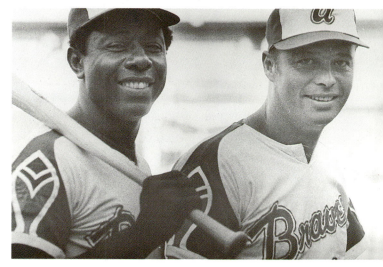

Mickey Mantle

Born: October 20, 1931; Spavinaw, Oklahoma
Height: 5'11½"   Weight: 195
Batted left-handed and right-handed, threw right-handed
Elected to the Hall of Fame in 1974

In the spring of 1951, 19-year-old Mickey Mantle, already acclaimed for his amazing speed and awesome bat, came north from Florida with the New York Yankees. When he hit poorly in April and May, manager Casey Stengel sent him to the Yankee minor league team in Kansas City. "I was a bigger bust there than I'd ever been with the Yankees," Mantle once told free-lance writer John Devaney.

One night, after Mantle had gone 0-for-5, his father, Elvin ("Mutt") Mantle, a former semipro player and zinc miner who was dying of Hodgkin's disease, paid his son a surprise visit. "After we talked for a while," said Mantle, "he got into his car. 'Dad,' I said to him, 'I might as well go home with you. I'll never be able to hit major league pitching.'

"He turned and stared at me. 'All right,' he said, 'get in. If you've got no more guts than that, you don't belong in the big leagues.'

"My face turned red," Mickey said. "I stepped back from the car. Dad drove home alone that night. I went back to my hotel and thought about what he had said. He'd embarrassed me. But he made me realize something. If I could hit, I'd make the Yankees. If I couldn't—well, I'd find that out too."

Mickey began to hit. Within a few weeks, he was back with the Yankees. He started in right field, next to Joe DiMaggio, in the 1951 World Series. A year later, he took over for DiMaggio as the Yankee center fielder. "I don't think I could have made it without my dad," Mantle has often said.

Mickey Mantle was more than merely the most feared power hitter of the 1950s and much of the 1960s, a talent who threatened to hit the ball out of the park every time he came to the plate; he was the dominant player of his time. During his 18-year career, he led the league in homers four times. His highest total came in 1961, when he had 54, finishing second to Roger Maris, who hit his record 61 that season. Mantle had 536 career homers. Other accomplishments include ten seasons batting more than .300, four slugging titles, three MVP awards,

Mantle and Roger Maris battled for the home run title in 1961. Maris, with 61 homers, won. Mantle ended with 54. (Wide World)

and the 1956 Triple Crown, with 52 home runs, 130 RBIs, and an average of .353.

Mantle achieved all that he did despite a career that was of relatively short span. For instance, Mantle played in merely 2,401 games, compared to 3,298 for Hank Aaron and 3,026 for Stan Musial. Mantle had 8,102 at bats, to Aaron's 12,364 and Musial's 10,972.

The most powerful switch-hitter ever, Mantle is said to be responsible for the term "tape measure" home run. In 1953, he walloped a pitch in Washington's old Griffith Stadium that soared beyond ordinary limits. An enterprising Yankee employee, armed with a tape measure, hunted the ball down and reported it had traveled 563 feet.

Other of Mantle's tape-measure homers included a 550 footer in Chicago's Comiskey Park that, according to Yankee manager Casey Stengel, left seats "flyin' around for five minutes." And while no major leaguer has ever hit a fair ball out

Mantle supplanted DiMaggio as Yankee center fielder in 1952. (Wide World)

of Yankee Stadium, Mantle came very close. A drive of his in the "old" stadium caromed off the facade above the right field stands, 390 feet from home plate at a point 106 feet above the ground.

Mantle's own choice as his most memorable home run was a ninth-inning, game-winning blast against St. Louis in game three of the 1964 World Series. It was his sixteenth Series homer, breaking Babe Ruth's record. (Mantle finished with 18 homers in Series competition; Ruth had 15.) In his 18 years with the team, the Yankees won 12 pennants.

Besides his raw power, Mantle was fast, at least in the early stages of his career. When batting lefty, he could race from home plate to first base in a blazing 3.1 seconds. But a succession of injuries robbbed him of his speed.

In the 1951 World Series, Mantle, chasing a fly ball off of Willie Mays's bat, tripped over a drain, tearing a ligament in his right knee and ending up in the hospital. That was his "good" knee. The left had been damaged earlier by osteomyelitis. His knees, arm, and shoulders pained him through most of his career.

"I see him swing sometimes," Boston outfielder Carl Yastrzemski once said, "and even from the outfield you can see the knee buckle under him and the way he winces in pain, I wince, too."

"When he runs, he's in pain all right," said then Cleveland shortstop Dick Howser. "But what amazes me, he runs so hard even though he must know that one bad step and his career is all over, shot, finished."

Despite his achievements and the superstar status he held almost from the beginning of his career, Mantle was for many years unpopular with the fans. They seemed to feel he was not a worthy successor to the great DiMaggio. They booed him for striking out and he struck out a great deal. It

took a full decade before Mantle was accepted as a Yankee hero in the tradition of Ruth, Gehrig, and DiMaggio.

In the years following his retirement, Mantle has become much more of a hero than he had ever been as a player. In Dallas, where he lives, he plays golf and does public-relations work for a bank. He operates a successful restaurant in New York. And at baseball card and memorabilia shows where he sometimes appears, Mantle receives as much as $40 for signing his name. Only one or two other players ever commanded so large an amount.

On the baseball-card circuit, Mantle receives as much as $40 for his signature. (George Sullivan)

OPPOSITE: Because of injuries, Mantle often played in pain. Here he swings—and winces. (Wide World)

31

Willie Mays

Born: May 6, 1931; Westfield, Alabama
Height: 5'10½"   Weight: 170
Batted right-handed, threw right-handed
Elected to the Hall of Fame in 1979

One of the most exciting players in baseball history, Willie Mays dazzled fans with his explosive hitting, daring baserunning, and electrifying fielding plays. He led the National League in slugging five times and belted 660 home runs in his 22-season career, ending third on the all-time home run list behind Hank Aaron and Babe Ruth. But neither Aaron nor Ruth ever approached Mays in all-around ability. One piece of evidence: Mays was the first player to become a member of the 300-300 club—300 home runs, 300 steals.

When Mays joined the New York Giants in 1951, a horrendous batting slump had him in tears. But manager Leo Durocher stuck with him. Before long, Mays, at 20, was a key member of the team that rallied late in the season to win the pennant, but lost to the Yankees in the World Series. Mays ended up as the National League's Rookie of the Year.

Mays spent most of 1952 and all of 1953 in the army. He returned to the Giants in 1954 to hit .345

and wallop 41 home runs. The Giants won the pennant again and faced Cleveland in the World Series. In the first game, Mays made what has been called the most famous catch in baseball history—a breathtaking back-to-the-plate, over-the-shoulder grab of a world-class wallop off the bat of Vic Wertz.

Mays's personality and style wove a legend in New York. He was adored for his zestful manner, his basket catches, and the way his hat flew off when he pursued fly balls. When the Giants moved to San Francisco after the 1957 season, it was different for Mays. San Franciscans were a little bit cool to him.

But Mays won them over. And no wonder. He hit 49 home runs and drove in 141 runs in leading the Giants to a pennant in 1962. He hit 52 homers in 1965 and captured MVP honors for the second time.

Mays played 16 years in San Francisco (and only five years for the Giants in New York). He had his

The most famous catch in baseball history—Mays's back-to-the-plate, over-the-shoulder grab of Vic Wertz's 425-foot drive in the 1955 World Series. (Wide World)

career-high seasons in homers, RBIs, and runs scored while playing there, and he hit his 500th and 600th homers while wearing a San Francisco uniform. In 1972, when he learned he had been traded to the New York Mets, he was saddened. He played one season for the Mets, then retired.

Mays finished among the leaders in most offensive categories. He ended his career with 1,903 runs batted in, 2,062 runs, and 3,283 hits. He batted over .300 10 times, including seven years in a row. He had eight straight seasons with at least 100 RBIs.

Mays went back to Candlestick Park in San Francisco late in the season of 1986 for a day honoring Willie McCovey. When the convertible carrying Mays came out onto the outfield grass, a great roar went up from the stands. For five minutes, the fans stood and cheered and cheered.

Mays's return to New York caused big headlines. (New York Post)

Ralph Kiner

Born: October 27, 1922; Santa Rita, New Mexico
Height: 6'2"   Weight: 195
Batted right-handed, threw right-handed
Elected to the Hall of Fame in 1975

Hank Aaron, Willie Mays, and Ted Williams may have hit more home runs than Ralph Kiner. But no one except Babe Ruth ever hit them more frequently. In his relatively short 10-year major league career, Kiner belted out 7.09 home runs in every 100 trips to the plate. (Ruth had a home run percentage of 8.50.)

And no player dominated the home run standings the way Kiner did. In each of his first seven seasons in the majors, Kiner either led or tied for the league leadership in homers. Babe Ruth never registered a streak of more than six consecutive seasons.

Big for his age and a natural athlete, Ralph was raised in California by his widowed mother. At Alhambra High School, he averaged almost one homer per game. At 18, he signed with the Pittsburgh Pirates for a $3,000 bonus and an additional $5,000 when he reached the major leagues.

Three years in the minor leagues followed and then Kiner served three years in the U.S. Navy as a bomber pilot. When he left the service, he was 6-foot-2, 195 pounds, and 24 years old.

As a rookie with the Pirates, one of the league's weaker teams, Kiner hit a pitiful .247 and led the league in strikeouts with 109. But the 23 home runs he hit were also tops in the league, enabling him to become the first rookie home run leader in 40 years.

Kiner was determined to improve. During his first two seasons, he noted on index cards every pitch thrown to him. By studying his records, Kiner came to an understanding of the strategy pitchers were using against him. He then developed counterstrategy. He also purchased a movie camera so his swing could be recorded on film for study. And he and a teammate spent so much time in extra batting practice that the two chipped in to buy a car for their pitcher.

Kiner also benefited when the Pirates swung a deal that brought 36-year-old Hank Greenberg to Pittsburgh for what was the last active year of his career. Despite the 11-year difference in their ages, the two became close friends and roommates. Greenberg encouraged Kiner and gave him countless batting tips.

After Greenberg retired, Greenberg Gardens, the area in left field in Forbes Field where he had aimed his home runs, was renamed Kiner's Korner.

Five times Kiner hit more than 40 homers in a season, and twice his total topped 50. He hit his peak in 1949 with 54 round-trippers, the second highest total in National League history.

Kiner earned $90,000 in 1951, top salary in the National League. This caused a teammate, Fritz Ostermueller, to comment: "Home run hitters drive Cadillacs; singles hitters drive Fords." In the years since, the remark has often been credited to Kiner himself.

Kiner was traded to the Chicago Cubs in 1953, a deal that shocked Pittsburgh fans. Two years later, he found himself in the American League with the Cleveland Indians. After hitting 18 homers in 1955 despite being bothered by a painful disc problem in his back, Kiner decided to retire. He served as general manager of the San Diego Padres, then members of the Pacific Coast League, from 1955 until 1960.

Two years later, when the New York Mets were being organized, Kiner became the club's radio and TV broadcaster. He has remained behind the TV mike in New York for decades, becoming one of baseball's most durable voices. Besides his play-by-play responsibilities, Kiner also hosts a post-game interview show. It is named, appropriately, "Kiner's Korner."

In 1953 and 1954, Kiner played for the Chicago Cubs. In this photo, Joe Garagiola serves as catcher. (Wide World)

Besides his home run feats, Kiner also has won acclaim as a New York Mets' broadcaster. (Wide World)

Stan Musial

Born: November 21, 1920; Donora, Pennsylvania
Height: 6'   Weight: 180
Batted left-handed, threw left-handed
Elected to the Hall of Fame in 1969

The Cardinals' Stan Musial made his first big league appearance in a Sunday doubleheader against the Cubs and rapped out four straight hits. On the last of the hits, he went to second on an infield out. After a walk, the next batter dumped the ball in front of the plate. The catcher pounced on it and fired to first. The umpire called the runner safe, but the catcher and first baseman protested. Musial, meanwhile, kept right on running. He crossed the plate before the Cubs realized what was happening, scoring on a ball that had traveled perhaps ten feet. After Musial finished the day with two more hits and a couple of diving catches in the outfield, Cub manager Jimmie Wilson shook his head in disbelief. "Nobody could be that good," he said.

Stan Musial was "that good" for 22 years. Between 1941 and 1963, Musial won seven league batting championships, six slugging titles, and three MVP awards. For his career, Musial averaged .331, homered 475 times, and set more than 50 league hitting records.

The fifth of six children born to Polish miner Lukasz Musial and Czech American Mary Lancos, Musial was a star performer in baseball and basketball at Donora High School in Donora, Pennsylvania. The University of Pittsburgh offered him a basketball scholarship. The Cards wanted him to sign a baseball contract. When Stan confessed he wanted to go with the Cards, his father said no, insisting his son get a college education.

Stan's mother came to his defense. "Why did you come to America?" she asked her husband.

"Because it's a free country," he answered.

"All right," she said. "And in America a boy is free *not* to go to college, if that's his choice."

Mr. Musial couldn't argue with that. Stan was allowed to sign with St. Louis.

Throughout his career, Musial used an odd, curled-up, peekaboo batting stance, the barrel of the bat sticking almost straight up in the air. As this suggests, Musial was not a slugger in the tradition of free-swinging Babe Ruth. In fact, he never won a home run crown. Yet he got the job done. In his first four seasons, all pennant-winning seasons for the Cardinals, Musial specialized in doubles and triples and won the first two of his batting crowns.

In 1948, Musial suddenly developed into a home run hitter, averaging 30 or more home runs for the next 10 years. And he continued to hit big bunches of doubles and triples. In fact, only Hank Aaron surpasses Musial in extra-base clouts. Aaron had 1,477 extra basers; Musial, 1,377.

In 1962, at the age of 41, Musial was still slugging the ball. He hit .320 that season, which was third best in the league. In 1963, he retired. Not long after, a huge sculpture of Musial was erected outside of Busch Memorial Stadium in St. Louis and, in 1969, his first year of eligibility, Musial was elected to the Hall of Fame.

Musial hit his 300th home run in 1955. When he retired eight years later, he had 475 of them. (Wide World)

Musial poses at first base during his rookie year of 1942. (Wide World)

Ted Williams

Born: August 30, 1918; San Diego, California
Height: 6'4"   Weight: 200
Batted left-handed, threw right-handed
Elected to the Hall of Fame in 1966

All Ted Williams ever really wanted to do was to hit better than anyone else. And he pretty much achieved that goal. With the possible exception of Babe Ruth, there has been no better pure hitter in baseball history.

Tall and lean, quick-tempered and opinionated, the Splendid Splinter carved out a statistical record that no hitter has been able to match. He had a .344 career batting average, with 521 home runs. His .634 slugging percentage is second only to Babe Ruth's.

Williams won six American League batting titles, one of them the celebrated .406 in 1941. He won four home run titles, including his personal high of 43 in 1949. Four times he led in RBIs, nine times in slugging average. Twice he won the Triple Crown.

Williams's grandest season was 1941, when he was only 23. He batted .406, becoming the last player to reach the .400 level. On the final day of the season, Williams's average stood at .399955, meaning that he could have sat and settled for a rounded-off .400. But he insisted on playing. The Red Sox faced the Philadelphia A's in a double-header. In his first at bat, Williams lashed a single, followed by a home run. In all he went 4 for 5 in the first game. In the second game, he went 2 for 3, which gave him his .406.

He also led the league with 37 homers and a .735 slugging average that year. And in the All-Star game, Williams hit a three-run homer with two out in the ninth inning for a thrilling 7-5 American League victory.

In the Most Valuable Player voting that year, however, Joe DiMaggio, who had hit safely in 56 consecutive games, edged out Williams. Many fans thought Williams had been slighted. Ted himself felt that he had been passed over because of his less than harmonious relationship with the press, which bestows the honor in a vote among baseball writers. This belief was reinforced in 1947 when

OPPOSITE: Tall and lean, Williams was nicknamed the Splendid Splinter. (Wide World)

Williams won the Triple Crown and again saw Di-Maggio capture MVP honors. One Boston writer left Williams completely off the ballot. However, Williams did manage to win MVP honors in 1946 and 1949.

Born in San Diego, Williams learned to play baseball on the city's playgrounds and sharpened his skills at Herbert Hoover High School. At 17, he signed a contract with the San Diego Padres of the Pacific Coast League. After seeing Williams play, Eddie Collins, general manager of the Red Sox, purchased his contract. The Sox assigned Williams to their Minneapolis farm team in 1938, where he slugged 43 homers and hit .366 to lead the league. Williams opened the 1939 season as Boston's right fielder. Later he switched to left field.

Williams and Joe DiMaggio frequently competed for the sport's spotlight. (*Sport* magazine)

Williams never won any awards as a defensive player. Sometimes he would fail to back up infielders on grounders or not move fast enough on fly balls. One day about a month after he had joined the Sox, Williams let a ground ball slip through his legs. When he turned to run after the ball, some fans felt he moved too leisurely and began hurling insults at him. Williams yelled insults back.

After another bad incident, Williams vowed, "I'll never tip my hat to them again." And he never did. Whenever he hit a home run, Williams would circle the bases with his head down, then duck into the dugout. No matter how long or how loudly the crowd cheered, no acknowledgment ever came from Williams. Even when he hit a homer in his last turn at bat before retiring, he did not relent.

There were other examples of Williams's lack of maturity. He would sometimes fling his bat high into the air when he failed to get a hit. There were incidents with fans involving obscene gestures and spitting.

Hitting was all that Williams seemed to care about. He treated it as though it were a science. When Williams was beginning his big league career, he sought advice from Rogers Hornsby. "What do I have to do to be a good hitter?" Williams asked. "Get a good ball to hit," Hornsby replied.

Williams followed that advice with the greatest determination, disciplining himself to swing only at those pitches that were in his "happy zone"—where he could hit .400 or better. He seldom swung at a low-percentage pitch.

His discerning eye at the plate also helps to explain why Williams led the American League in walks seven times and is second only to Babe Ruth in career walks. Discipline at the plate is also what enabled Williams to say: "I had a higher percentage of game winning home runs than Ruth; I was walked more frequently than Ruth and struck out less—once in eleven times up to Ruth's one in six. I had to be doing something right, and for my money the principal thing was being selective."

What Williams achieved is all the more impressive when it's realized that his career was twice interrupted by military service. A marine pilot, Williams lost three years in World War II and most of two additional seasons during the Korean War.

Williams's slugging heroics continued throughout the 1950s. At the age of 40 in 1958, with an average of .328, Williams became the oldest player to capture a batting title. He batted .316 in 1960, his final season. At Fenway Park on his last trip to the plate, Williams clouted an emotion-packed homer.

Williams retired to his comfortable home on Islamorada in the Florida Keys to spend most of his time fishing. But in 1969, he was lured back to

Williams was 51 when he tried managing, a profession he seldom enjoyed. (George Sullivan)

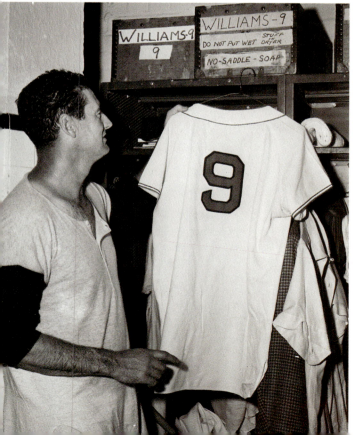

Williams hangs up his number 9 uniform for the last time in the dressing room at Fenway Park. The date: September 28, 1960. (Wide World)

manage the Washington Senators by the principal owner, Robert Short. At first, Williams was successful, steering the Senators to a fourth-place finish and earning Manager of the Year honors. But modern-day players taxed Williams's patience and he came to call managing a "pain." He gave it up in 1972.

Beginning in 1978, Williams began serving as a batting instructor at the Red Sox camp in Winter Haven, Florida, each spring. He would arrive at the complex each day before 9:00 A.M. and spend a full day working with the young players. He fully realized, however, that sometimes the best advice is no advice at all. "When I was comin' up," Williams once told *New York Times* sports columnist Ira Berkow, "Lefty O'Doul said to me, 'Don't let anyone change you.'" That *was* good advice.

41

Joe DiMaggio

Born: November 25, 1914; Martinez, California
Height: 6'2"   Weight: 193
Batted right-handed, threw right-handed
Elected to the Hall of Fame in 1955

While Joe DiMaggio, the Yankee Clipper, had a lifetime batting average of .325, twice led the league in batting, with .381 in 1939 and .352 in 1940, and had that fabled batting streak of 56 consecutive games, don't be misled. DiMaggio was no singles hitter; he was a slugger. He had quick wrists, the widest stance of anyone in baseball, and, in his early years at least, he pulled the ball in a manner that became a trademark.

There's statistical evidence, too. With a career slugging average of .579, Joltin' Joe is number six on the all-time list. And although he lost three years to service in the army, he still ended his career with 361 home runs. His top season for homers was 1937 when he hit 46, and he led the league that year and again in 1948.

Born in Martinez, California, and brought up in San Francisco, DiMaggio first came to fame with the San Francisco Seals of the Pacific Coast League. After he hit in 61 consecutive games for the Seals in 1933, major league clubs started bidding frantically for his contract. But one day early in 1934, jumping off a bus, Joe twisted his knee and ankle badly and his leg had to be put in a cast. Most teams lost interest in him as a result. Not the Yankees. Despite his "bad" knee, the Yanks landed DiMaggio for five players and $25,000. He never played for any other team.

DiMaggio's best year was probably 1939, when he hit .381, the highest average of his career, and had 126 RBIs, as the Yankees won their fourth consecutive pennant. Indeed, in the DiMaggio years, it was almost taken for granted that Yankees would win the American League title. In his 13 seasons with the team, DiMaggio missed the World Series only three times.

DiMaggio's fielding won him as many tributes as his hitting. He covered the broad expanse of the Yankee Stadium outfield with long, loping strides. He always arrived at where he was going before the ball but he never seemed to have to hurry to get there. He had a strong arm, too, until it was weakened by injury.

Handsome and quiet, DiMaggio was named to

the American League All-Star team 13 times. He was the league's MVP three times—in 1939, 1941, and 1947.

A bone spur in his heel and other painful injuries blighted the final stages of his career. When his batting average slipped to .263 in 1951, the Yankee Clipper decided to quit, even though he was offered big money to play in 1952. He married Marilyn Monroe, sold coffeemakers on television, and was voted greatest living player by a panel of sports writers. Except for an occasional public appearance, he now lives the quiet life of an American folk hero.

In 13 seasons with the Yankees, DiMaggio missed playing in the World Series only three times. Here he celebrates with teammate Hank Bauer following the Yanks' series win over the Giants in 1951. (Wide World)

Johnny Mize

Born: January 7, 1913; Demorest, Georgia
Height: 6'2"   Weight: 220
Batted left-handed, threw right-handed
Elected to the Hall of Fame in 1981

When Johnny Mize was in his prime, John Lardner of *Newsweek* praised him with these words: "He can pull the ball, but he also has power in all directions. He owns sharp eyes and enough plate intelligence to be a consistent hitter. The pitchers in the league fear no man as much, and that is the ultimate tribute."

A big, burly, red-faced man with a strong and graceful swing, Mize, the Big Cat, used that power and intelligence to win or share four home run titles and three RBI crowns. In 1947, he became one of a handful of sluggers to hit 50 or more home runs in a season when he hit 51, still the National League record for lefties.

Mize was born and grew up in Demorest, Georgia, a town so small, he once said, a good-size crowd could cause the place to tilt. He didn't become seriously interested in baseball until he was attending Piedmont College in Demorest. Mize also played for several town teams. The Cardinals sent a scout to take a look at him, and the scout liked what he saw. After signing, Mize toiled in the minors for six years. He was 23 when he was called up to play first base for the Cardinals in 1936.

A mild-mannered young man, Mize joined a club that was anything but. A team of wild men and jokers, they were called the Gas House Gang. "Their uniforms are stained and dirty and patched and ill-fitting," wrote Frank Graham in the *New York Sun.* "They don't shave before a game and most of them chew tobacco. They are not afraid of anybody—enemy ballplayers, fans, umpires, club owners, league officials. . . ."

It all agreed with Mize. His six years in St. Louis were among the best of his career. He led the league in slugging three times, averaged well over 100 RBIs each year, and hit well above .300.

After Mize, a straightaway hitter, was traded to the Giants in 1941, he had to adjust his swing to the short right field fence in the Polo Grounds. He hit a good many long drives to center that were 400-foot outs. But adjust he did. The 51 home runs he hit in 1941 were evidence of that.

Mize, with teammates Enos Slaughter (center) and Pepper Martin, at spring training camp in the late 1930s. (National Baseball Hall of Fame & Library)

In all his years with the Cards and Giants, Mize was frustrated by not ever having a chance to appear in a World Series. That situation changed in 1949 after he was sold to the Yankees, where he became a part-time first baseman and full-time pinch hitter. In his five years with the club, 1949–1953, the Yanks won the World Series five times. In 1952, Mize became the second man in Series history to pinch-hit a home run.

Despite his many achievements, Mize was overlooked by the Hall of Fame voters for more than two decades. In 1981, the Veterans' Committee finally voted him in. In his acceptance speech, Mize said: "Some people have asked me if going through the Veterans' Committee was like going through the back door, but I said no. Look at the Veterans' Committee, with Hall of Fame players on it. These are my peers. That makes me proud."

Mize got his 2,000th hit shortly before his retirement in 1953. His lifetime total is 2,011. (National Baseball Hall of Fame & Library)

Hank Greenberg

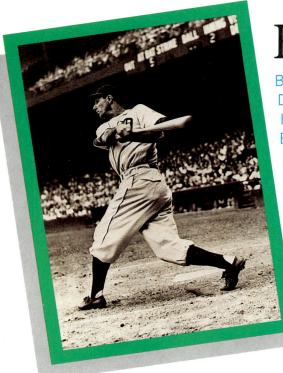

Born: January 1, 1911; New York, New York
Died: September 4, 1986
Height: 6'3½"   Weight: 215
Batted right-handed, threw right-handed
Elected to the Hall of Fame in 1956

In the early 1930s, when Babe Ruth was still slugging home runs for the New York Yankees, Hank Greenberg was beginning to hit them for the Detroit Tigers. In 1935, the year the Babe called it quits, Hammerin' Hank tied with Jimmie Foxx for the American League lead in homers with 36. Then he, along with Foxx, Ted Williams, Lou Gehrig, and Joe DiMaggio, continued to pace the major leagues in home runs until World War II.

In 1938, Greenberg threatened one of Ruth's most notable records, his single-season record of 60 homers. Hank hit 58 that year. No right-handed hitter ever hit more. (Jimmie Foxx, also a righty, hit 58 in 1932.)

Number five on the all-time slugging list with a .605 average, Greenberg led the American League in home runs four times and RBIs five times, despite the classy competition. He hit .300 or better every full season of his career, except the last one, 1946, when he averaged .277. He had a lifetime average of .313.

Greenberg and Lou Gehrig had careers that were similar. Both were raised in New York City and worked hard to achieve baseball success. Both became first basemen who made life miserable for American League pitchers.

And both men played with diligence and determination. In 1940, at the peak of his career, Greenberg agreed to switch to the outfield so the Tigers could use Rudy York, another fearsome slugger, at first base. The experiment worked better than anyone expected. Detroit won the pennant and Greenberg was named the league's MVP (for the second time).

Early the next year, 1941, with World War II at hand, Greenberg was drafted into the army. He didn't rejoin the Tigers until 1945, missing four full seasons. In his first appearance, 47,729 turned out to welcome him at Briggs Stadium. Greenberg smashed a homer and went on to bat .311 with 13 homers that season, spearheading the Tigers' drive for the pennant.

On the final day of the season, Detroit needed one more win to clinch. Greenberg delivered a mammoth grand slam homer in the ninth inning that carried the Tigers to victory. It was one of the most dramatic home runs in baseball history.

The following year, 1946, after leading the league in homers, with 44, and RBIs, with 127, Greenberg was sold to the Pirates. Hank heard the surprising news on his car radio.

At Pittsburgh, Greenberg's greatest impact was as a teacher. He roomed with a young slugger named Ralph Kiner, who later credited Greenberg's instruction and example for much of the success he attained as a home run hitter.

After his retirement as a player, Greenberg enjoyed a successful career as a baseball executive, helping to bring a league championship to Cleveland and later to Chicago. In the early 1960s, he left baseball to devote more of his time to his interests on Wall Street and the tennis court.

Hank Greenberg, a New Yorker from Greenwich Village who starred for the Detroit Tigers. (Detroit Tigers)

With the exception of Jimmie Foxx, Hank Greenberg hit more home runs from the right side of the plate than any other player in baseball history. (National Baseball Hall of Fame & Library)

Josh Gibson

Born: December 21, 1911; Buena Vista, Georgia
Died: January 20, 1947
Height: 6'1"   Weight: 215
Batted right-handed, threw right-handed
Elected to the Hall of Fame in 1972

The Black Babe Ruth is what they called Josh Gibson. Burly and broad shouldered, Gibson, a catcher, clouted home runs of tremendous length. One, hit at Washington's Griffith Stadium, was measured at 575 feet. Another is said to have been the only fair ball ever hit out of Yankee Stadium, soaring over the upper deck in left field.

Born in 1911 on a small Georgia farm, Josh was raised in Pittsburgh, where the family moved when he was 13. He learned to play baseball on the city's playgrounds. At the time, black players were barred from playing in the all-white major leagues. While young Josh was a fan of the Pittsburgh Pirates, he had no hope of ever signing a contract with the team. His ambition was to play for the Homestead Grays, Pittsburgh's team in the Negro American League. As a stepping-stone Josh played with all-black amateur and semipro teams in the Pittsburgh area.

One summer evening when Josh was 18, the fabled Kansas City Monarchs came to Pittsburgh to play the Grays. Joe Williams, a fastballer, was to pitch for the Grays that night. But early in the game, the Homestead catcher, complaining that he couldn't see Williams's fastballs because of the poor lighting, walked off the field. Judy Johnson, the Homestead manager, had seen Gibson catch and knew he was in the stands. He signaled him to come down to the field. The crowd of 30,000 waited while Gibson got into his uniform. That night he launched his professional baseball career.

Playing in the Negro leagues was a scruffy, ragtag business. Teams traveled by bus and sometimes played two games in the same day in different cities. There'd be a day game, followed by a 40 or 50 mile bus ride, then another game under lights. On Sundays, teams would sometimes play three games. When the season was over, black players continued to toil in the Mexican leagues or in the Caribbean.

In an interview with Donald Honig, author of *Baseball When the Grass Was Green,* James ("Cool Papa") Bell, a Negro league star for more than two decades, once described Gibson as "one of the greatest you ever saw." Said Bell: "Ruth used to hit them *high*. Not Gibson. He hit them *straight*. Line drives, but they kept going. His power was to center field, right over the pitcher's head. I played against Foxx. But Gibson hit harder and further more often than Foxx or any other player I ever saw."

Records were poorly kept in the Negro leagues. Thus, in statistical terms, at least, no one knows what Gibson accomplished. In league and semipro games in 1931, he was credited with 75 home runs. His batting average for 17 years with the Grays and Pittsburgh Crawfords was over .350 and he is believed to have topped .400 at least twice.

When, in 1946, Jackie Robinson was signed by the Brooklyn Dodgers as the first black player in the major leagues, Gibson was 35 and in poor health. Embittered that he had been passed over in favor of Robinson, Gibson died the next year.

In 1972, a special committee was established to place stars of the Negro leagues in the Hall of Fame. Satchel Paige, perhaps the greatest black pitcher of all time, was the committee's first choice. Josh Gibson was second.

Gibson could also hit for average and is believed to have topped .400 at least twice. (National Baseball Museum and Hall of Fame)

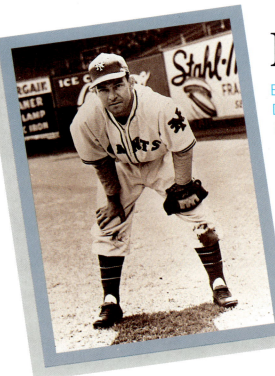

Mel Ott

Born: March 2, 1909; Gretna, Louisiana
Died: November 21, 1958
Height: 5'9"   Weight: 170
Batted left-handed, threw right-handed
Elected to the Hall of Fame in 1951

Mel Ott arrived in New York in 1925 at the age of 16 with a straw suitcase and a peculiar batting style. He stayed to become one of the most popular players in New York Giant history and the first National Leaguer to hit 500 home runs.

Ott's batting style was like no other. A lefty, he took his stance with his feet wide apart. As the pitcher released the ball, Ott would hoist his right leg, then drop it quickly as he lashed out with his bat.

When Ott tried out for Giant manager John McGraw, he made a stunning impression with his ability to golf the ball down the line and into the handy upper deck of the Polo Grounds, 256 feet away. (Almost two-thirds of Ott's home runs would be hit at home.) While McGraw felt his teenage slugger needed seasoning, he decided to keep Ott on the major league club rather than allow a minor league manager or coach to tinker with his batting style.

During the 1925 season, Ott just sat and watched. The next year, he appeared in 35 games as a backup outfielder. In 1927, when McGraw more than doubled Ott's playing time, he batted .282 and hit an inside-the-park home run, his first of 511 homers, a National League record at the time Ott retired.

Ott also set National League records for runs batted in, runs scored, and walks. Most of his records stood until the 1960s. The record for bases on balls, broken by Joe Morgan, lasted until 1982.

Six times Ott led the league in walks and 10 times he was issued 100 or more. Four times he drew five walks in one game. The first time was on the final day of the 1929 season in a game against the Philadelphia Phillies. Ott had 42 home runs that year; so did Chuck Klein of the Phillies. Philadelphia pitchers walked Ott five consecutive times, once with the bases loaded, so he wouldn't have a chance to outdo Klein. The strategy worked. Klein, with 43 homers, won the home run title. But in the years that followed, Ott would capture the homer crown six times.

Ott hit .389 in the 1933 World Series and won

Ott was the first player in National League history to hit 500 home runs.
(Copyright *Washington Post;* Reprinted by permission D.C. Public Library)

the fifth and deciding game with a tenth inning homer. The Giants were Series participants again in 1936 and 1937 and Ott homered in each, although the Giants lost to the Yankees both times.

In 1942, when Ott was approaching the final seasons of his career as a player, Giant owner Horace Stoneham assigned him to take over as manager, a job he held for six years. In 1947, he led the team to fourth place, which was the best he was able to do. His critics said he was too soft, too lax. In fact, when Leo Durocher, who succeeded Ott as field boss, made his famous statement, "Nice guys finish last," it was Mel Ott to whom he was referring.

Jimmie Foxx

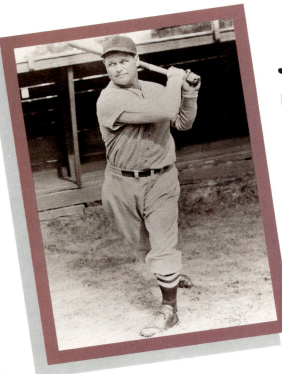

Born: October 22, 1907; Sudlersville, Maryland
Died: July 21, 1967
Height: 5'11½"   Weight: 190
Batted right-handed, threw right-handed
Elected to the Hall of Fame in 1951

They called Jimmie Foxx Old Double X for the way he spelled his name, and the Maryland Strong Boy because of his broad chest and heavily muscled arms. And he was also known as the Beast, a nickname he got for his ability to send a baseball skyrocketing as far as any human before or since.

Foxx's drives were not long flies. He belted the ball hard and straight, according to outfielder Roger ("Doc") Cramer, a contemporary. "Once I saw him hit a ball in Chicago, a line drive against the center-field fence, and he had to slide into second base," Cramer once told Don Honig. "The ball was hit so hard that when Luke Appling went out to get the relay, it bounced right back into his glove. He turned and threw, and Foxx just made it—and Jimmie could run. That's how hard Foxx could hit."

Not only did Foxx hit them hard, he hit them often. In 20 major league seasons, he clubbed 534 home runs, which places him number eight on the all-time list, just ahead of Ted Williams and only two homers behind Mickey Mantle.

In 1932, Foxx hit 58 homers, his all-time high, and one of four times he led the league. Perhaps more impressive, he holds the record for consecutive years in which a batter hit 30 or more homers. Foxx did it 12 times.

He got at least one home run in every World Series in which he played, and he played in three of them—in 1929, 1930, and 1931. At various times in his career, he led the American League in almost every department that had anything to do with slugging.

Friendly and high spirited, Foxx developed those big muscles by plowing, milking, and doing other chores as a Maryland farm boy. While he liked baseball as a teenager, he had no ambition to become a major leaguer. But one day when he was 16 and playing as a catcher for Easton (Maryland) in the Eastern Shore League, Foxx was spotted by Frank ("Home Run") Baker, who had won legendary fame as a member of the Philadelphia A's. At Baker's urging, the Athletics signed Foxx. Because the Philadelphia team had a topflight catcher in

Mickey Cochrane, Foxx learned to play first base and later third.

In 1928, at the age of 20, Foxx became an everyday player for the A's. He batted .328 that year and hit 13 home runs.

After the 1935 season, the A's dealt Foxx to Boston, where he continued his exceptional hitting. Not until 1942 did his career start heading downhill. Twice he led the league in hitting and he ended his career with an overall average of .325.

Despite his easygoing personality, Foxx was fearsome at the plate. He cut off the sleeves of his uniform to show his big muscles. When he dug in, eyed the pitcher, and raised his bat, those muscles bulged and rippled. "One day my glasses fogged up while I was pitching to him," Lefty Gomez once recalled, "but when I cleaned them and looked at the plate and saw Foxx clearly, it frightened me so much I never wore them again."

Besides playing first base, Foxx caught and played third.
(National Baseball Hall of Fame & Library)

Lewis ("Hack") Wilson

Born: April 26, 1900; Elwood City, Pennsylvania
Died: November 23, 1948
Height: 5'6"   Weight: 195
Batted right-handed, threw right-handed
Elected to the Hall of Fame in 1979

For half a dozen or so years during the late 1920s and early 1930s, the Cubs' Hack Wilson was the foremost slugger in the National League. Fans loved to watch him take his turn at the plate. In typical slugger fashion, Wilson swung from the heels, the result being a long home run or a maddening miss. If he missed, Wilson would explode in fury and slam his bat to the ground. In all cases he put on a grand show.

In 1930, Wilson had one of the finest seasons ever enjoyed by any player. By the end of August, he had accumulated 44 home runs to break the National League record of 43 set the year before by Chuck Klein. He had also broken his own RBI record. In the final month of the season, Wilson got even hotter. He ended with 56 home runs and 190 runs batted in. The home run total is still the National League record and the RBI total is the major league mark. Wilson's .723 slugging average was also tops in the league that year.

Hack Wilson didn't look like a baseball player. He was short and very muscular—a fireplug. Be-

cause he was said to resemble George Hackenschmidt, a famous wrestler of the day, he was given the nickname Hack.

His career in organized professional baseball began when he was 21 and graduated from local amateur leagues in eastern Pennsylvania to the Martinsburg, West Virginia, club in the Blue Ridge League. After two years at Martinsburg as a catcher and a year in Portsmouth, Virginia, as an outfielder, Wilson moved up to the New York Giants.

He was a sensation with the Giants in 1924, and by midseason was hitting in the .370s. But an ankle injury slowed him down and his average plummeted. When the slump continued the next season, the Giants sent him back to the minors. The Cubs picked him up in 1926 for the bargain price of $5,000.

Wilson's days of glory were at hand. Right from the beginning, he started hitting homers and driving in runs. From 1926 through 1930, Wilson led the National League in home runs four times and drove in 100 or more runs five times. He was outstanding in 1929, hitting 39 homers, with 159 RBIs, and .345 batting average, and the Cubs won the pennant. Wilson batted a stunning .471 in the World Series, but the Cubs lost to the A's in five games. In 1930, Wilson was even better. To go with his 56 homers and 190 RBIs, he had a .356 batting average.

In 1931, Rogers Hornsby took over as manager of the Chicago team. Wilson and the hard-nosed Hornsby didn't get along. Wilson sulked and drank too much. When his batting average fell to .261 and his homer output plunged to 13, the Cubs packed Wilson off to the Brooklyn Dodgers. Wilson made a modest comeback in 1932, finishing with 23 homers and 123 RBIs. But the great days were over. By 1935, he was playing in the minor leagues once more. Although Wilson earned a total of about $250,000 during his career, he died penniless at 48, a victim of alcoholism.

Wilson was never known for his diving catches. In 1929, he posed—unconvincingly—for this publicity photo. (New York Public Library)

Lou Gehrig

Born: June 19, 1903; New York, New York
Died: June 2, 1941
Height: 6'1"   Weight: 212
Batted left-handed, threw left-handed
Elected to the Hall of Fame in 1939

"I'm not a headline guy," mild-mannered, raw-boned Lou Gehrig once said. And he was right. When Gehrig hit .545 in the 1928 World Series, Babe Ruth hit .625. When Gehrig smacked a home run at Wrigley Field in the 1932 Series, Ruth, batting ahead of him, had just hit his "called shot" homer. Gehrig's feat was all but overlooked.

When Gehrig hit four homers in a game and just missed a fifth because of a brilliant catch, the deeds were accomplished on the very day that John J. McGraw stepped down as manager of the New York Giants. That story dominated the papers the next morning.

Gehrig wasn't a money guy, either. In 1927, when he hit 47 homers and was named the American League's Most Valuable Player, he earned $6,000. That same year Babe Ruth hit 60 home runs and got paid $40,000.

The Yankees signed the 20-year-old Gehrig, a Columbia University student, in 1923. His contract called for a $1,500 bonus and a $3,000 salary. Scout Paul Krichell convinced Yankee owner Ed Barrow to make the investment by telling him, "I think I saw another Babe Ruth today."

Although he played in Ruth's shadow for much of his career, Gehrig established records that no other player, not even Ruth, could touch. During his career, Gehrig hit 23 homers with the bases loaded, a major league record. Gehrig led the American League in RBIs five times, achieving some extraordinary totals. In 1927, he had 175, and in 1930, 174. In 1931, he knocked 184 runs across the plate, the all-time high for the American League. His average of .92 runs batted in per game is another Gehrig mark (one that he shares with Hank Greenberg and Sam Thompson). Gehrig ended his career with 1,990 runs batted in, third behind Ruth and Aaron.

Some critics say that Gehrig's RBI statistics have an inflationary quality because he batted fourth in the Yankee lineup, behind Ruth. Ruth was thus frequently on base when Gehrig came to

While Ruth was the great crowd pleaser, Gehrig inspired the Yankees and was the team's captain.
(National Baseball Hall of Fame & Library)

bat. Perhaps. But it's also true that Gehrig often came up with the bases empty because Ruth had cleared them.

Gehrig won the Triple Crown in 1934, batting .363 with 49 homers and 165 RBIs. He was the American League's MVP four times, in 1931, 1934, 1936, and 1937.

While every list of great sluggers places Gehrig within the top three, his most notable baseball achievement has to do with durability. On June 1, 1925, in a game against the Washington Senators at Yankee Stadium, Gehrig was sent up to the plate to pinch hit for Pee Wee Wanninger. The next day, Gehrig played first base. The next game Gehrig missed was May 2, 1939. He played almost 14 years without a break, a total of 2,130 games. No wonder he was nicknamed the Iron Horse. Of all of baseball's most important records, most observers feel that Gehrig's consecutive-game streak is the most likely to last forever.

Gehrig's career total of 1,990 RBIs is second only to Ruth's and Hank Aaron's.
(New York Yankees)

Gehrig died at the relatively young age of 38 of amyotrophic lateral sclerosis, now commonly called Lou Gehrig's disease. In 1939, with death approaching, a day was held in Gehrig's honor at Yankee Stadium. He told the more than 60,000 fans, "You've been reading about my bad break for weeks now. But today I think I'm the luckiest man alive."

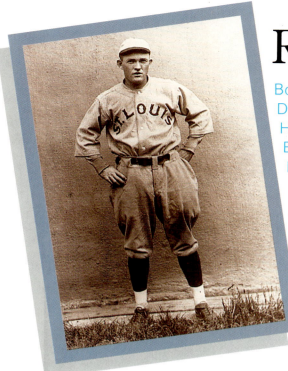

Rogers Hornsby

Born: April 27, 1896; Winters, Texas
Died: January 5, 1963
Height: 5'11½"   Weight: 200
Batted right-handed, threw right-handed
Elected to the Hall of Fame in 1942

Rogers Hornsby is often called the greatest right-handed batter in baseball history. He hit .400 or better three times and his .424 average in 1924 is the record for the century.

While those extraordinary accomplishments overshadow his deeds as a long-ball hitter, Hornsby ranks right up there with Joe DiMaggio, Willie Mays, and Hank Greenberg as one of slugging's all-time greats. Ten times Hornsby led the National League in slugging. He led in home runs twice, in triples twice, and in RBIs four times. In combining average with power, Hornsby had no equal.

Hornsby batted from a unique stance. He stood with his feet together as deep in the batter's box as he could get, then swung freely. He hit frozen ropes, line drives that made even brave infielders tremble. The ball would keep rising, sailing over the head of any outfielder not playing deep. Hornsby never read or went to the movies, fearing the exertion would impair his batting eye.

The Rajah, as he was nicknamed, joined the St. Louis Cardinals in 1915 as a third baseman and shortstop. Not until 1920 did he settle down at second base, where he became known for his quickness and throwing accuracy on double plays.

Hornsby won the National League batting title seven times and ended with a .358 career mark. Only Ty Cobb hit for a higher lifetime average. Hornsby also won two Triple Crowns and two MVP awards.

Hornsby never won any popularity contests, however. He was often gruff and insensitive, with little regard for the feelings of others. Boston columnist Dave Egan said he was "born to be a target."

In 1926, when Hornsby served as player-manager of the Cardinals, he steered the team to the pennant and a World Series win over the Yankees. He was 30 years old and at the peak of his career. But he feuded often with Cardinals owner Sam Breadon, who subsequently dealt his superstar to the New York Giants. In return, the Cards received New York's great second baseman Frankie Frisch and pitcher Jimmy Ray. It was one of the most famous trades in baseball's first half century.

Hornsby didn't get along any better in New York than he had in St. Louis. Boston, where he batted .387 in 1928, was the next stop, and another short one.

Moving on to the Chicago Cubs in 1929, Hornsby batted .380 with 39 homers and won the National League's MVP award, his second. He then managed the Cubs for a time, returned to the Cardinals in 1933, and later that same season managed their crosstown rivals, the St. Louis Browns. In the years thereafter, the Browns finished eighth, sixth, seventh, seventh, and eighth with Hornsby at the helm.

A long and difficult exile in the minor leagues followed. There were stopovers at Chattanooga, Oklahoma City, Fort Worth, Beaumont, and Seattle (in the Pacific Coast League at the time). Hornsby coached for the Chicago Cubs in 1958 and 1959 and was a coach for the New York Mets in 1962, their first season. He was 66.

Except for the pennant he won in 1926, Hornsby never had much success as a manager. It may have been that he was too cold and outspoken. Still, as Brooklyn catcher Clyde Sukeforth once observed, "When he had a bat in his hand, he had nothing but admirers."

Hornsby stood as deep in the batter's box as the rules allowed, then swung freely.
(National Baseball Hall of Fame & Library)

Babe Ruth

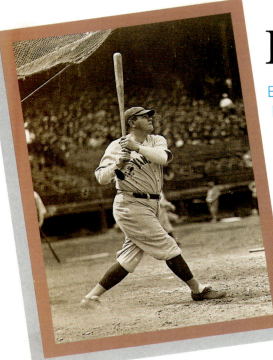

Born: February 6, 1895; Baltimore, Maryland
Died: August 16, 1948
Height: 6'   Weight: 215
Batted left-handed, threw left-handed
Elected to the Hall of Fame in 1936

Babe Ruth was the first great slugger in baseball history. Until Babe Ruth, baseball's offense was based on singles, sacrifice bunts, and stolen bases. Teams played for one run at a time. Ruth, by hitting more and longer home runs than anyone dreamed possible, transformed the game. Other hitters copied Ruth in seeking to bury the opposition with one all-or-nothing swing. The big hit, the big inning became the objective.

The hitter who was to revolutionize baseball began his career as a left-handed pitcher with the Boston Red Sox in 1914. His record was 18-8 in his first season, 23-12 as a sophomore, and 24-17 his third year. (Complete games occurred at least twice as frequently in those days.) Yet his hitting was as impressive as his pitching, and in 1918 he was made a part-time outfielder so he could get to the plate more often. The next season, Ruth clouted 29 homers, breaking a record that had been on the books for 35 years.

Ruth was dealt to the Yankees in 1920, arriving the same year that the spitter and other trick pitches were banned. He hit 54 homers in his first year with the club. Only one other *team* hit more than 50 homers that season, and the entire American League had only 370.

In 1927, Ruth had 60 homers to break his record of 59 set in 1921. That mark stood until 1961, when Roger Maris, also a Yankee, hit 61 homers in a season that was eight games longer.

In total, Ruth led the league in home runs 12 times, in RBIs six times, in runs scored eight times, and in bases on balls 11 times.

Ruth was the leader in slugging 12 times, including an .847 average in 1920, the highest in history. His .690 career slugging average is second to none.

Ruth's other career totals include: 714 home runs (a record topped by Hank Aaron in 1974), 2,211 RBIs, 2,174 runs, 2,056 walks (the all-time record), and a .342 batting average. He struck out 1,330 times, which places him 31st on the all-time list.

It wasn't merely all those home runs that made

Ruth poses cheerfully with Boston Braves infielder Walter ("Rabbit") Maranville. (New York Public Library)

of the batter's box, lifted one finger, and said, "That's one."

Root delivered again for strike two. Again Ruth stepped out, held up two fingers, and said, "That's two." Then Ruth took his bat and pointed it toward the center field bleachers. Root wound up and threw. Ruth took a mighty swing and drilled the ball deep into the seats. Miraculously, he had "called his shot."

Born in Baltimore in 1895, George Herman Ruth was brought up in a poor, rough section of the city. His birthplace is now a landmark, the Babe Ruth Birthplace Museum. Neither of his parents devoted much time to George, and he seldom went to school, preferring to roam the streets. "I was a bum as a kid," he once told columnist Bob Considine.

Babe Ruth quite possibly the most famous athlete the nation has produced. His colorful personality and flair for the dramatic were as important as his hitting ability.

Both of those qualities were exhibited in what is perhaps the most memorable incident of Ruth's career. It took place during the 1932 World Series, the Yankees versus the Cubs. The Yanks won the first two games. In the third contest, played at Wrigley Field, Ruth came to bat in the fifth inning against Charlie Root, after homering earlier. The crowd greeted him with loud boos. Root pitched and the Babe swung and missed. Ruth stepped out

RUTH ENJOYS RAZZING CUBS

Raises His Fingers To Show Strike Count, Then Hits Homer

HERMAN HOLDS PACE

Has Got On Base First Time At Plate In Every Game

[By the Associated Press]

Chicago, Oct. 1—Babe Ruth stole the third show of the World Series today and had the time of his life doing it.

As he belted ball after ball into the bleacher seats during batting practice he kept up a rapid-fire conversation with the awe-stricken Cubs.

"You've had your last look at the stadium (meaning Yankee Stadium)," he shouted to Pat Malone. "You good-hearted guys, why I've got more money than all of you."

When he was eight, George was placed in St. Mary's Industrial School, a reform school for unruly boys. Sports were very important at St. Mary's. The approximately 800 boys there took part in track, boxing, and wrestling. Baseball teams were organized on all levels. Ruth pitched, caught (despite being left-handed), and played third base. At 18, he was the biggest boy in the school and the best baseball player, known even then for his long and frequent home runs.

Jack Dunn, the owner and manager of the Baltimore Orioles, a minor league team at the time, went to St. Mary's to scout Ruth. Two weeks later he signed him to his first contract. The veteran players called the young rookie "Babe," and the newspapers and fans picked it up.

In 1920, Ruth's first year with the Yankees, the team became the first in baseball history to attract one million fans for a season. (New York Public Library)

In 1914, the same year he signed Ruth, Dunn peddled him to the Boston Red Sox. Within two years, Ruth was the best left-handed pitcher in the league. In the 1916 and 1918 World Series, Ruth pitched 29 ⅔ consecutive scoreless innings, a record that stood until 1961. But Babe was even more impressive as a hitter, and so began playing regularly in left field. As an outfielder, he would bat more often.

After Babe joined the Yankees in 1919, his popularity skyrocketed. The Polo Grounds, where the Yankees played their home games until 1923, was often filled to capacity. In 1920, Ruth's first year with the club, the Yankees became the first team in baseball history to draw one million fans for a season.

Ruth played on his first of seven Yankee pennant winners in 1921, the year of the first Yankee World Series. He was always at his best in World Series competition. He hit four home runs in the 1926 Series, batted .625 in the 1928 Series, and set a career record of 15 Series homers (later broken by Mickey Mantle).

The Yankees released Ruth after the 1934 season and he ended his playing career with the Boston Braves in 1935. In retirement, Ruth bowled and golfed. He played himself in the movie, *Pride of the Yankees,* based on the life of Lou Gehrig.

In 1946, Ruth learned he had cancer. A day was held in his honor at Yankee Stadium in 1948. Two months later he died.

Since his death, the Babe Ruth mystique has flourished. Among collectors, his autograph is more highly prized than that of any other player. "A Ruth signature is worth $450," says Herman Darvick, a noted autograph dealer. "You can buy Hank Aaron's for about $15, and Roger Maris's is worth about the same." There's a special Babe Ruth Room at the National Baseball Hall of Fame and Museum and his name is frequently included in American history textbooks. Few deny he was the greatest hero baseball has produced.

Ruth crosses home plate after hitting his 60th home run in 1927. (National Baseball Hall of Fame & Library)

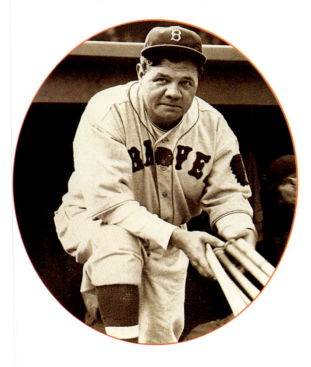

Ruth ended his career in 1935, playing for the Boston Braves. (National Baseball Hall of Fame & Library)

John Franklin ("Home Run") Baker

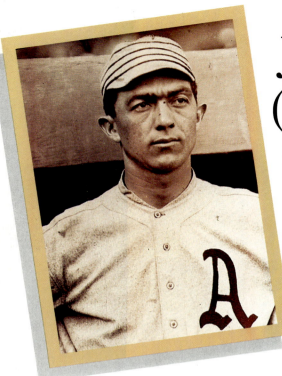

Born: March 13, 1886; Trappe, Maryland
Died: June 28, 1964
Height: 5'11"   Weight: 173
Batted left-handed, threw right-handed
Elected to the Hall of Fame in 1955

The most home runs Frank Baker ever hit in his career was 12. That was in 1913.

And for his career, Baker had 93 round-trippers. Sluggers today get that many in a couple of seasons.

Why, then, was he called *Home Run Baker?*

He deserved it. He was the best homer hitter of his day, leading the American League in home runs for four consecutive years—with 11 in 1911, 10 in 1912, 12 in 1913, and 9 in 1914.

Baker happened to play during a period in baseball when pitchers held sway, thanks to the rules that allowed the use of spitballs and other trick pitches. Big Ed Walsh, the best of the spitballers, won 194 games in a 14-year career, with an earned run average of 1.82, the lowest in baseball history. Home runs were as rare as triple plays.

A powerfully built farm boy from Maryland's Eastern Shore, Baker, a third baseman, looked like he might be awkward and slow moving. But he was deft as a fielder and fast enough to steal as many as 40 bases one season and more than 200 during his career.

Baker came close to never having a major league career. In 1907, after five games at third base for the Baltimore Orioles, an Eastern League team at the time, Baker was judged to be too clumsy and was released. A season at third base for Reading (Pennsylvania) in the Tri-State League followed. Although he batted .229 and had six homers, no one seemed to be interested in him; no one, that is, except Connie Mack, owner of the Philadelphia A's. Mack purchased Baker from the Reading team in 1908 and the next season he took over at third base.

Baker acquired his nickname in the 1911 World Series. The A's faced the tough New York Giants, who had Christy Mathewson and Rube Marquard, two of the best pitchers in baseball history, throwing for them. Mathewson had won 26 games in 1911; Marquard, 24.

The biggest crowd in World Series history up to

When Baker hit his first grand slam in 1909, it was the talk of the baseball world for days.
(National Baseball Hall of Fame & Library)

that time, 38,381, packed the Polo Grounds for the first game to watch the Giants behind Mathewson win, 2-1. In the sixth inning of the second game, Baker blasted a two-run homer off one of Marquard's fastballs, a drive that carried the A's to a 3-1 victory.

The next day, Mathewson faced the A's a second time and carried a 1-0 lead into the ninth inning. After Mathewson had retired the first batter, Baker slammed a fadeaway pitch into the right field stands, tying the score, 1-1. The A's went on to win in the eleventh inning, 3-2, and eventually to win the Series, four games to two.

After those home runs off of New York's pitching aces, Frank Baker became known as Home Run Baker. The nickname clung to him until his death, at 78, in 1963.

While Baker achieved his greatest fame during his seasons with the A's, from 1908 to 1915, he also played six years with the New York Yankees. But he enjoyed playing baseball anywhere, in small towns as well as big cities. In 1915, he refused to report to the Athletics, preferring to stay on his farm in Trappe, Maryland, and play baseball for a semipro team in Upland, Pennsylvania. In 1920, while under contract with the Yankees, Baker spent another season farming and playing semipro ball. "Some people wonder why I'm content to play with a farmer team," he said. "The game of baseball itself is what interests me. Baseball is baseball anywhere—and I love it."

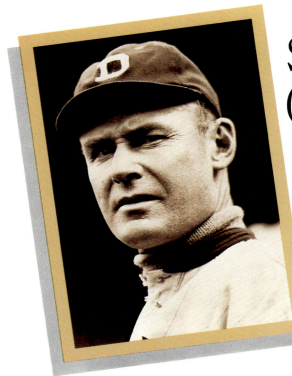

Samuel Earl ("Wahoo Sam") Crawford

Born: April 18, 1880; Wahoo, Nebraska
Died: June 15, 1968
Height: 6'   Weight: 190
Batted left-handed, threw left-handed
Elected to the Hall of Fame in 1957

Called Wahoo Sam because he was born in Wahoo, Nebraska, Sam Crawford was the outstanding power hitter of the dead-ball era, the period, that is, before the introduction of the cork-center baseball at the end of the 1910 season. Crawford is to the three-base hit what Hank Aaron is to the home run, hitting more triples than any player in history, and he holds the distinction of being the only player to have led both leagues in home runs.

A tall, hard-muscled young man with oversize hands, Crawford was a powerful line drive hitter. Though not particularly fast, he ran the bases with good sense, stretching many a double into a triple. His record of 312 triples during his 19-year career is not likely to be broken. Willie Mays, for example, who was rather a modern-day version of Crawford, punched out a total of 140 triples in 22 major league seasons. And José Canseco, a bigger, more powerful version of Crawford, averages a mere two or three triples a season.

When it came to home runs, Crawford led the National League in 1901 with 16, and the American League in 1908 with seven.

Born in 1880, Sam was the son of the town barber, and a career as a haircutter loomed for him. But it was a tough way to make a living. Barbering in those days meant standing on your feet from seven in the morning until after dark. You got ten cents for a shave, a quarter for a haircut. When Sam got a chance to play baseball for $65 a month, plus free lodging, for the Chatham club in the Canadian League, he jumped at it. After the Canadian League folded, Sam caught on with Columbus (Ohio) of the Western League. From there, he was transferred to Grand Rapids (Michigan). Before the season ended, Sam was purchased by Cincinnati, where he became a favorite of the fans. They were saddened when he left in 1903 to join Detroit.

Sam usually played right field for the Tigers, flanking Ty Cobb. Davy Jones, in left field, was later replaced by Bobby Veach. The Crawford-

Cobb-Veach combination came to be rated as one of the best outfields of all time. They were agile on the bases, solid hitters, and performed in the outfield like a well-oiled machine.

At the plate, Crawford earned a reputation as a "hard out." Even when the pitcher managed to retire him, Sam usually hit the ball so hard he could have just as easily ended up a base runner. "None of them can hit them quite so hard as Crawford," Fielder Jones, center fielder for the Chicago White Sox, once said. "He stands up at the plate like a brick house; there's no moving him away from it. And he hits all the pitchers without playing favorites. When he's hitting, they all look alike."

Sam led the American league in triples five times and the National League once. His 26 three-base hits in 1914 is an American League record (that he shares with Shoeless Joe Jackson).

After his major league career came to an end in 1917, Sam spent four years with Los Angeles in the Pacific Coast League. There he continued to pound the ball, smacking a league-leading 21 triples in 1920 and averaging .318 in 1921. After the 1921 season Crawford retired. When he was named to the Hall of Fame in 1957, he requested his nickname, Wahoo Sam, be placed on his memorial plaque.

A powerful line drive hitter, Crawford is the only player to have led both major leagues in home runs.
(National Baseball Hall of Fame & Library)

Roger Connor

Born: July 1, 1857; Waterbury, Connecticut
Died: January 4, 1931
Height: 6'2"   Weight: 210
Batted left-handed, threw left-handed
Elected to the Hall of Fame in 1976

Everyone knows it was Babe Ruth's record that Hank Aaron cracked on his way to hitting 755 home runs. But whose record did Ruth wipe out when he swept to his total of 714?

The answer: Roger Connor's.

From Waterbury, Connecticut, Roger Connor was one of baseball's first long-ball hitters, a home run king of the 1880s and 1890s. In a major league career that spanned 18 seasons, Connor belted the old dead ball for four bases 131 times (some sources say 136 times). Connor's record stood until 1921, when the Babe buried it.

The powerful Connor simply muscled the baseball out of the park. He was tall and broad, a big man for his day. A contemporary described him in these terms: "He is as fine a specimen of physical development as any in the profession, being a few inches over six feet in height, weighing over two hundred pounds, without an ounce of superfluous flesh, and being admirably proportioned."

When Jim Mutrie took over the operation of the New York club in the National League in 1885 and nicknamed the team the Giants, it's believed that Roger was his chief inspiration, the man he had most in mind.

In a game at the old Polo Grounds at 110th Street and Fifth Avenue in Manhattan in 1887, Roger blasted a home run over the right field fence that won billing as the "longest hit ever made in this city." Never before had a ball been driven out of the Polo Grounds.

Connor twice led the National League in homers, with 17 in 1887 and 14 in 1888. He shared the home run title in the Players League (see below) in 1890 when he hit 13 round-trippers.

Roger Connor was one of eight children of Irish immigrants who settled in Waterbury. His younger brother, Joe, also played professional baseball, although his career lasted only four years. Another brother, Dan, was the chief grounds keeper at the Waterbury ballpark.

Roger's first appearance in organized baseball came in 1876, when he caught on with the Monitors of Waterbury. He was 18 years old and al-

Nearly 6-foot-2 and weighing 210 pounds, Connor was one of the men the New York owner had in mind when he called his team the Giants.
(National Baseball Hall of Fame & Library)

ready a six-footer. Despite the fact he threw lefty, the Monitors installed him at third base. Connor played for the town team for two years before moving on to clubs in New Bedford and later Holyoke in Massachusetts. In games against Springfield, Holyoke's arch rival, Connor drove long home runs out of the ballpark into the Connecticut River.

In 1881, playing for Troy in the National League, Connor dislocated his shoulder, an injury that forced him to switch from third base to first. There he remained for the rest of his career. While Connor never won great renown as a fielder, he twice managed to lead the National League's first basemen in fielding percentage.

In 1890, Connor was one of the many players to leave their National League clubs to join teams in the newly formed Players' League, which had come into existence as a result of long-standing hostilities between players and owners over such contractual matters as the reserve clause and salary ceilings. Connor was a staunch supporter of the Players' League, which was forced to disband after one season. Connor went back to playing with the Giants in 1891, hitting seven homers and batting .293.

In 1897, Connor played his final season in the National League. He hit one homer, his 131st and last. In the years that followed, Connor operated teams in Massachusetts and Connecticut, but he was still playing first base in the minors at the age of 45. After he retired, he lived in Waterbury until his death at 74. He was chosen for the Hall of Fame in 1976, a full century after his first season with the Waterbury Monitors.

All-Time Records

This section presents listings of the lifetime leaders in statistical categories pertaining to sluggers. Of the several offered, slugging average is the most important, for it measures one's ability to hit for extra bases, which is the essential nature of slugging, after all.

A slugging average is determined by dividing at bats into total bases and carrying the result to three decimal places. (Total bases is the sum of bases on hits compiled by using this formula: one for a single, two for a double, three for a triple, and four for a home run.)

Here's an example: For the season of 1927, Babe Ruth had 540 at bats, with 95 singles, 29 doubles, 8 triples, and 60 home runs. His total bases amounted to 417 (95 + 58 + 24 + 240).

Dividing his at bats into his total bases gave him a slugging average of .772.

$$\begin{array}{r} .772 \\ 540\overline{)417.000} \\ \underline{378\ 0} \\ 39\ 00 \\ \underline{37\ 80} \\ 1\ 200 \\ 1\ 080 \end{array}$$

For a career, one's slugging average is figured in the same way—at bats are divided into total bases.

Babe Ruth holds the all-time single-season slugging average—.847, which he set in 1920. His lifetime slugging average is .690, also the record.

HOME RUNS

1. Hank Aaron	755	14. Mel Ott	511
2. Babe Ruth	714	15. Lou Gehrig	493
3. Willie Mays	660	16. Stan Musial	475
4. Frank Robinson	586	Willie Stargell	475
5. Harmon Killebrew	573	18. Carl Yastrzemski	452
6. Reggie Jackson	563	19. Dave Kingman	442
7. Mike Schmidt	548	20. Billy Williams	426
8. Mickey Mantle	536	21. Darrell Evans	414
9. Jimmie Foxx	534	22. Duke Snider	407
10. Willie McCovey	521	23. Al Kaline	399
Ted Williams	521	24. Graig Nettles	390
12. Ernie Banks	512	25. Johnny Bench	389
Eddie Mathews	512		

SLUGGING PERCENTAGE

1.	Babe Ruth	.690	14.	Hack Wilson	.545
2.	Ted Williams	.634	15.	Chuck Klein	.543
3.	Lou Gehrig	.632	16.	Duke Snider	.540
4.	Jimmie Foxx	.609	17.	Frank Robinson	.537
5.	Hank Greenberg	.605	18.	Al Simmons	.535
6.	Joe DiMaggio	.579	19.	Dick Allen	.534
7.	Rogers Hornsby	.577		Earl Averill	.534
8.	Johnny Mize	.562	21.	Mel Ott	.533
9.	Stan Musial	.559	22.	Babe Herman	.532
10.	Willie Mays	.557	23.	Ken Williams	.530
	Mickey Mantle	.557	24.	Willie Stargell	.529
12.	Hank Aaron	.555	25.	Mike Schmidt	.527
13.	Ralph Kiner	.548			

TRIPLES

1.	Sam Crawford	309	14.	Sam Rice	184
2.	Ty Cobb	294	15.	Edd Roush	183
3.	Honus Wagner	252	16.	Jesse Burkett	182
4.	Jake Beckley	243	17.	Ed Konetchy	181
5.	Roger Connor	233	18.	Buck Ewing	178
6.	Tris Speaker	223	19.	Rabbit Maranville	177
7.	Fred Clarke	220		Stan Musial	177
8.	Dan Brouthers	205	21.	Harry Stovey	175
9.	Joe Kelley	194	22.	Goose Goslin	173
10.	Paul Waner	190	23.	Tommy Leach	172
11.	Bid McPhee	188		Zack Wheat	172
12.	Eddie Collins	186	25.	Rogers Hornsby	169
13.	Ed Delahanty	185			

RUNS BATTED IN

1.	Hank Aaron	2,297	14.	Honus Wagner	1,732
2.	Babe Ruth	2,209	15.	Reggie Jackson	1,702
3.	Lou Gehrig	1,990	16.	Tony Perez	1,652
4.	Stan Musial	1,951	17.	Ernie Banks	1,636
5.	Ty Cobb	1,933	18.	Goose Goslin	1,609
6.	Jimmie Foxx	1,922	19.	Nap Lajoie	1,599
7.	Willie Mays	1,903	20.	Mike Schmidt	1,595
8.	Cap Anson	1,879	21.	Rogers Hornsby	1,584
9.	Mel Ott	1,860		Harmon Killebrew	1,584
10.	Carl Yastrzemski	1,844	23.	Al Kaline	1,583
11.	Ted Williams	1,839	24.	Jake Beckley	1,575
12.	Al Simmons	1,827	25.	Willie McCovey	1,555
13.	Frank Robinson	1,812			

DOUBLES

1.	Tris Speaker	793	14.	Joe Medwick	540
2.	Pete Rose	746	15.	Al Simmons	539
3.	Stan Musial	725	16.	Lou Gehrig	534
4.	Ty Cobb	724	17.	Al Oliver	529
5.	Nap Lajoie	657	18.	Cap Anson	528
6.	Carl Yastrzemski	646		Frank Robinson	528
7.	Honus Wagner	640	20.	Ted Williams	525
8.	Hank Aaron	624	21.	Willie Mays	523
9.	Paul Waner	603	22.	Ed Delahanty	522
10.	Charlie Gehringer	574	23.	Joe Cronin	515
11.	George Brett*	559	24.	Babe Ruth	506
12.	Harry Heilmann	542	25.	Tony Perez	505
13.	Rogers Hornsby	541		*Still active, 1991	

STRIKEOUTS

1.	Reggie Jackson	2,597	14.	Willie McCovey	1,550
2.	Willie Stargell	1,936	15.	Frank Robinson	1,532
3.	Mike Schmidt	1,883	16.	Willie Mays	1,526
4.	Tony Perez	1,867	17.	Rick Monday	1,513
5.	Dave Kingman	1,816	18.	Greg Luzinski	1,495
6.	Bobby Bonds	1,757	19.	Eddie Mathews	1,487
7.	Lou Brock	1,730	20.	Frank Howard	1,460
8.	Mickey Mantle	1,710	21.	Jim Wynn	1,427
9.	Harmon Killebrew	1,699	22.	Jim Rice	1,423
10.	Dwight Evans*	1,643	23.	George Foster	1,419
11.	Dale Murphy*	1,627	24.	George Scott	1,418
12.	Lee May	1,570	25.	Darrell Evans	1,410
13.	Dick Allen	1,556		*Still active, 1991	

WALKS

1.	Babe Ruth	2,056	14.	Eddie Collins	1,499
2.	Ted Williams	2,019	15.	Willie Mays	1,464
3.	Joe Morgan	1,865	16.	Jimmie Foxx	1,452
4.	Carl Yastrzemski	1,845	17.	Eddie Mathews	1,444
5.	Mickey Mantle	1,734	18.	Frank Robinson	1,420
6.	Mel Ott	1,708	19.	Hank Aaron	1,402
7.	Eddie Yost	1,614	20.	Tris Speaker	1,381
8.	Darrell Evans	1,605	21.	Reggie Jackson	1,375
9.	Stan Musial	1,599	22.	Willie McCovey	1,345
10.	Pete Rose	1,566	23.	Dwight Evans*	1,337
11.	Harmon Killebrew	1,559	24.	Luke Appling	1,302
12.	Lou Gehrig	1,508	25.	Al Kaline	1,277
13.	Mike Schmidt	1,507		*Still active, 1991	

Index